MW01612626

RESCUED HEARTS

RESCUED HEARTS

•

Betsy Rogers

Kann 10.95
AVALON BOOKS
NEW YORK

PRINTED IN THE UNITED STATES OF AMERICA
ON ACID-FREE PAPER
BY HADDON CRAFTSMEN, BLOOMSBURG, PENNSYLVANIA

With love, gratitude, and admiration, I dedicate this book to
my two heroes:
My mother, Doris Rogers, and my brother, Don Rogers.
Bring on the cream puffs, Mom—let's celebrate!

Chapter One

Erica Johansen's notes slid off her lap as the helicopter in which she was riding made a sudden, unscheduled dip. A shiver of alarm tingled in the pit of her stomach. She shot a nervous glance at Buzz, the pilot sitting beside her. He was staring at the instrument panel, worry lines creasing his brow.

Then, just as suddenly, the helicopter leveled back into normal flight.

"Wow, what was that all about?" asked Erica, leaning forward to retrieve her papers.

"I'm not sure," replied Buzz, shrugging.

His aviator sunglasses reflected the light patterns that were dancing on the chopper's transparent canopy. He looked up at the rotors as they sliced the air above him and his passenger.

"We seem to be all right now," he said. "I'll have the

1

mechanics check it out when we get back." He flashed Erica a lopsided grin. "That was a little too exciting for you, huh?"

Erica returned his bantering smile and relaxed in her seat. If Buzz said everything was okay, that was good enough for her. Whatever had caused that momentary glitch, he'd deal with it. She'd found that the veteran pilot, with his keen sense of humor and easygoing manner, was the ideal partner for this job. With him at the controls, Erica felt as safe as if she were flying the helicopter herself. She also found it endearing that Buzz kept a snapshot of his wife and two sons taped inside the chopper.

Buzz banked into a turn, giving his passenger a magnificent view of the Seattle skyline. Erica checked her watch. It was almost time to transmit her first traffic report of the morning.

Her gaze returned to the appealing landscape spread out below them. In all of her twenty-eight years, she'd never seen—except on her recent trip to Norway—such a perfect combination of sky, forested mountains, and water as she'd found in the Pacific Northwest. In fact, she mused, Puget Sound and 'The Land of the Fjords' looked very much alike.

A feeling of pleasure rippled through Erica as she recalled her decison to move to Seattle from Denver the previous year. Not only had she discovered a beautiful part of Washington State, but she'd realized her dream of becoming an airborne reporter. It was something she'd wanted ever since she'd received her communications degree and pilot's license.

"I hear you got on the Board of Antiquities," said Buzz,

breaking in on her thoughts. He was referring to a volunteer organization dedicated to preserving Seattle's historically important buildings. "Congratulations," he added.

"Thanks," said Erica. "I'm really pleased."

"So, which old building are you saving?" asked Buzz.

"I've taken on the Wagner House project," said Erica.

"Oh, that one," said Buzz, giving a low whistle. "Didn't I hear that a private investor is trying to buy it? He plans to tear down 'that old eyesore', as he calls it, and put up a fancy new building."

"You heard right," said Erica, looking down at the traffic flow. "I haven't met him—in fact, I don't even know his name—but I understand he's very determined. We'll definitely have a fight on our hands. But," she added, "what this guy doesn't know is that I will throw my own body in front of the wrecking ball before letting him or anyone else destroy that wonderful house."

"My goodness," said Buzz, lightly joshing her, "such passion for your adopted city and its dusty old mansions."

"I just found out that my great-grandfather once lived in the Wagner House," said Erica. "So I feel I have a personal stake in its preservation."

"Go get 'em, tiger," said Buzz, flashing an encouraging smile at his passenger.

Just then, a signal from Erica's headset told her that she would go on the air in two minutes. As the chopper vibrated around her, the blades whirring above, Erica's excitement began to mount. She always felt that way when she was flying, especially when she was at the controls herself. It was exhilarating to be up in the sky, watching the earth's varied landscapes slide away beneath her in a living counterpane of hills, valleys, rivers, and towns. Although she enjoyed working as a traffic reporter, she had to admit that it was the aspect of flying that really made her heart sing. In fact, almost any job would do, as long as it included some flying, for, in the air, Erica felt freer than she ever felt on the ground.

"It's in my blood," she spontaneously said to Buzz.

"What is?" he said, looking puzzled. "Saving old buildings?"

"I was thinking about flying," said Erica, laughing.

"Oh, yeah, that," said Buzz with a smile. "I know what you mean."

As she scanned the busy commuter lanes below, Erica's mind drifted back to her vacation in Norway, the homeland of another branch of her family tree. Meeting her only living relatives, some cousins in Bergen, had been the thrill of a lifetime. On the streets of Bergen, Erica, tall and long-legged, had often been mistaken for a native-born Norwegian herself. She certainly looked the part, with her classically high Nordic cheekbones, blond hair, and eyes as blue as a fjord.

The helicopter skimmed over Lake Washington. As always on such a clear July day, the Seattle lake was dotted with sailboats. Their canvases reminded Erica of white butterflies poised against a field of rippling blue satin.

"I think there's a problem down on the bridge," said Buzz, jerking his thumb toward the glittering water.

"Let's take a look," said Erica.

Buzz circled around to gain a better view. Just then, Erica received the signal to broadcast. Adjusting her mike, she began transmitting her report.

"Good morning, commuters," she said. "Erica Johansen here for radio station KMBR. It's a beautiful day in Puget Sound country, without a cloud in the sky. If you're headed south, have a glance at Mount Rainier. It's never looked more spectacular."

At that moment, Erica thought she felt the helicopter give an unaccustomed shudder. Buzz was staring down at the lake and didn't seem to have noticed, so she mentally shrugged off the sensation as another false alarm and returned to her report.

The chopper banked for a second close pass over the bridge. Now Erica could see the problem that Buzz had been talking about. She began filling in her listeners.

"There's a red convertible stalled in the westbound lanes of the Evergreen Point Floating Bridge, which has traffic backed up past Foster Island. I'll keep an eye on the situation and let you know when—"

Erica stopped abruptly as the chopper gave a series of sharp jolts. This time she knew that it hadn't been her imagination. She turned her head to look at Buzz, who was frowning at the instrument panel. His lips were pressed together in a hard, grim line.

"What's wrong?" said Erica, a little too loudly. Her mike was still on. Again she felt the stirrings of fear in her stomach and sensed a sudden dryness in her mouth.

"I don't know," said Buzz, "but I don't like it. I'm heading for the barn."

He began banking to the left, then Erica noticed that he was struggling to control the aircraft. Suddenly, the helicopter canted to one side and the blades overhead slowed sickeningly.

The chopper rapidly began to lose altitude. Icy fingers of panic played an ominous tattoo along Erica's spine. She flailed out with both hands to brace herself as the helicopter lurched into a halting spiral toward the lake. Loud grinding noises erupted from the engine compartment. For a moment, Erica thought she was going to be sick.

"We're out of control!" yelled Buzz. "Mayday! Mayday! We're going down!" he shouted into his mike.

He was frantically trying to regain control of the aircraft, but it was obvious that his efforts were in vain. He uttered an oath of frustration and looked over at his partner.

"Hang on, Erica," he said, an urgent note in his voice. "This is going to be a rough landing."

"Isn't there anything you can do?" cried Erica.

The helicopter tipped over even farther. Everything that was loose in the small enclosure—pencils, papers, a map of Seattle, a spare headset—clattered into the nose of the chopper, which was now aiming for the water.

"I don't think so," Buzz shouted back. His arms trembled violently as he fought to hang on to the controls. "Better brace yourself!"

Erica was aware of several things during the last few moments that the chopper was aloft. The world spun around them and the cobalt-blue waters of Lake Washington were rushing up to meet the aircraft, which was falling like a stricken dragonfly. Her palms felt slick with sweat, and she could hear a ringing in her ears. She pushed out with her feet in an involuntary, and quite useless, attempt to brake their descent.

Then a wave of nausea welled up in her throat as she realized with chilling horror that she and Buzz were probably about to die. How could they survive a helicopter crash?

She caught a momentary glimpse of a nearby sailboat. There was a patch of blue on board. Perhaps it was a flag or some laundry hung out to dry. Erica's mind was in a muddle as the confusing images revolved beneath the chopper. Then she saw that the spot of color seemed to be a man wearing a blue sweater. He was shielding his eyes and staring up at the plummeting aircraft. Erica thought she could imagine the man's feelings of appalled helplessness as he watched the chopper go down.

She barely registered those details, however, as she realized that the helicopter was heading straight for the floating bridge. She could see the disabled red convertible amidst long lines of stalled cars and trucks. A fist of terror squeezed her heart and the blood pounded in her head. Her and Buzz's chances for survival were slim, at best, but they'd have no chance at all if they plowed into that solid expanse of metal and concrete.

"Hit the water, Buzz!" screamed Erica. "Don't hit the bridge! Hit the water! Hit the wa—"

There was a deafening crash as the chopper abruptly ended its erratic tumble from the sky. Erica's screams were snatched from her throat and she heard Buzz give a grunt, as though he'd had the wind knocked out of him. The whine of wrenching metal, as if being twisted by giant hands, filled the small compartment. Static sizzled from Erica's receiver, reminding her of hot grease on a griddle.

The sun-drenched light of a summer morning blanked out as the helicopter began sinking into a world of eerie blue dusk. With a grim sense of irony, Erica realized that although they'd landed in the water and she'd survived the initial impact, she was about to drown instead, trapped inside the chopper as it dove toward the bottom of Lake Washington.

For the first time in her life, Erica felt an overwhelming sensation of claustrophobia. She clawed at her safety harness as cold water began pouring into the cockpit. Her feet thrashed out, sending bits of paper and other floating debris into a crazy swirl. Erica noted with sadness that Buzz's family snapshot was bobbing around her ankles. Buzz himself was limp and silent beside her. Was he alive or dead?

Just then the chopper tilted to one side and gave her a glimpse of the dark and hostile depths beneath them. Erica cried out her anguish. She'd never before known such primal fear, such mindless panic. A spasm of regret went through her, as well. What a shame to die now, when there was still so much she wanted to accomplish.

There was another squeal of ripping metal as the helicopter continued to break apart. Erica felt something hard hit the back of her head. She groaned with pain. Then a feeling of numbness crept over her and she stopped struggling. Her hands fell away from where she'd been trying to wrench open the hatch on her side, and her head lolled against the seat.

The last thing Erica was aware of were the silver bubbles that were swirling around the outside of the cockpit. Fascinated, she stared with dimming vision at the bubbles floating upward in a universe of blue.

She could feel water lapping against her chest by that time, but all she could think about were those pretty bubbles. They reminded her of an illustration in a book she'd loved as a child, a book about water sprites. Those clouds of silver bubbles were fairies that were dancing just for her.

Smiling, she reached out to capture a bubble. If she could hold one of those little water fairies in her hand, somehow everything would be all right.

Her mind went black.

Chapter Two

Water . . . blue, blue water burnished with streaks of
silver . . . lily pads floating on the surface . . . the calm,
sweet light of a summer sun turning the air to gold . . .

Erica blinked her eyes and stared at the beautifully
framed Claude Monet print of lily pads on a pond hanging
on the wall opposite her bed. The soft blanket that covered
her felt warm and comforting beneath her still hands. A
peaceful silence surrounded her.

As consciousness slowly unfolded in Erica's mind, she
looked around in confusion. What had happened to her?
And why was she in a luxurious hotel suite?

The spacious room was decorated in restful, muted tones
of mauve and ivory. Several art prints, in addition to the
one of Monet's pond, graced the walls. A pair of easy
chairs stood on either side of an elegant table and lamp.
Double glass doors at one end of the room led out to a

sunlit balcony with blue sky beyond. Pink and white impatiens and some tender green ferns grew in planters on the balcony.

There were more flowers in the room, their fresh, delicate fragrance scenting the air. Erica's mind was still in a fog. Where had the flowers come from? she wondered. They were obviously gifts. One display in particular caught her eye. It was a lavish bouquet of blue irises, their long, regal stems emerging gracefully out of a lovely Chinese vase.

Erica closed her eyes as her head began to throb. Her hands clutched at the blanket and she gulped for air. She was remembering now. The whole terrifying scene replayed in her mind . . . the nauseating spiral downward as the helicopter lurched out of control, the blurred image of the man on the sailboat, their near miss of the congested bridge, and the chilly plunge into Lake Washington.

Buzz! What had happened to Buzz? Erica had somehow miraculously survived the crash, but what about her co-worker?

An intense feeling of urgency swept over Erica. Her eyes flew open and she tried to sit up. She had to find out what had happened to Buzz! Then she sank back down onto the pillow as her vision swam and the painful hammering in her head intensified.

She reached up to touch her forehead and felt bandages. Then she noticed that an intravenous tube was taped to her arm, and that there was a nurse's trolley beside her bed. Somewhere in the background she heard a muffled message being broadcast over a public-address system. She looked around again in puzzlement. Was she in a hotel or a hospital? Nothing made any sense.

If this was a hospital, reasoned Erica, there must be a nearby button, which she could use to summon a nurse. She'd just found the button and was about to press it when a tall, attractive man wearing green surgical scrubs entered the room. Filled with relief, Erica watched him stride toward her bed. Maybe he could answer the questions that were crowding her brain.

"I see you're awake, Ms. Johansen," he said. "How do you feel?"

His voice was low and deep, a pleasant sound. It stirred Erica's interest, reminding her of distant thunder promising dramatic weather.

"I'm confused," said Erica, "and sore all over. My head hurts and I'm very tired." She attempted a smile. "Aside from all that, Doctor . . ." Her voice trailed off.

"Moncrieffe," he filled her in. "I'm Dr. Grayson Moncrieffe."

The name resonated with power and presence. The man himself projected those same qualities, mused Erica. She watched him briefly return her smile as he gazed down at her from beside her bed. The lightweight fabric of his scrubs did little to conceal his physique. Erica noted with a ripple of admiration his broad chest, wide shoulders, and lean hips. Beneath his surgeon's garb, she sensed a masculine form that was toned and healthy, a result of regular outdoor exercise, she guessed. Very nice.

She continued her assessment as he picked up her chart. Dr. Moncrieffe's thick dark hair and handsome full mustache were lightly sprinkled with premature gray. Erica judged him to be a little over six feet tall and about thirty-four years of age. His eyes were his most arresting feature. Their rich shade of brown reminded Erica of vintage cognac, the sensuous French brandy that slips down one's throat like liquid silk, spreading fire in its wake.

The doctor looked vaguely familiar, but Erica's befuddled mind couldn't begin to sort out where she may have met him. Surely, she should remember the details of an encounter with a man endowed with such disarming good looks, she mused.

Dr. Moncrieffe studied Erica's chart, his wide, intelligent brow knitted in concentration. Then he nodded his head and glanced at her.

"This looks fine," he said, replacing the chart. "You can have some real food today, instead of this stuff." He motioned toward the IV drip.

"Great," said Erica. Then the questions started pouring out of her. "Where am I, anyway? At first I thought I was in a hotel, then I realized it was a hospital. Where did all these flowers come from? What happened after the crash? And what about—"

Grayson Moncrieffe laughed and held up his hand to halt her verbal avalanche.

"Whoa, slow down, Ms. Johansen," he said, "or I'll think you're trying to make up for the last two days of silence in one fell swoop."

"Two days of silence?" Erica was more confused than ever. "What do you mean?"

The doctor took her hand in a reassuring grasp that was warm and strong. Erica could imagine his hands performing an infinite variety of tasks, from the painstaking details of lifesaving surgery to the masculine ritual of shaving.

Feeling herself color, she dropped her eyes, surprised by her thoughts. If she wasn't careful, she'd make the adolescent blunder of forming a crush on her doctor—not a good idea.

"Hey, don't worry," said Dr. Moncrieffe, obviously misreading her reaction. The rich timbre of his voice washed over Erica like a current of soothing summer air. "You're going to be okay.

"Yes, you're in a hospital," he went on to explain. "You've been unconscious for a while because of a nasty blow to the head, which caused a concussion. That, plus some superficial scrapes and bruises, are all you got." He paused. "You were incredibly lucky."

Erica's lips began to tremble as she felt tears pooling in the corners of her eyes. She recalled the snapshot of Buzz's wife and children swirling at her feet. The sound of Buzz's groan as the helicopter hit the water and the sight of his limp form beside her replayed in her memory. She dreaded asking the question, but she had to know. In a voice that quavered with emotion, she spoke.

"What about—what about Buzz, my pilot? Was he lucky, too?"

"Yes, he was," said Dr. Moncrieffe, squeezing her hand. "It got pretty exciting there for a while, but he made it, as well."

He grinned. His eyes crinkled attractively at the outer corners, and his teeth gleamed white and even beneath his mustache.

"That pilot is one tough hombre," he went on. "He was actually cracking jokes when he got here. He has a broken arm and a couple of fractured ribs, but he'll be all right. He sends you his best, by the way."

"What a relief," breathed Erica and blinked away her tears.

There was a short pause as she digested the welcome news about Buzz's survival, then she continued her queries.

"Now what about those two days of silence you mentioned?" she asked in a hesitant tone. "What—what day is this?"

"It's about noon on Wednesday."

"Let's see," she said, staring at the ceiling as she calculated, "we crashed early Monday morning." She looked back at Dr. Moncrieffe. "And I've been lying here unconscious since then?" She struggled to comprehend the gap in her memory, for it made her feel helpless and even more disoriented than she already was.

"Pretty much," he said. "Oh, you faded in and out a little, but basically you've been out."

"I can hardly believe it," said Erica in wonderment. "What a weird sensation to lose a couple of days of my life and not even be aware of it."

"Don't let it bother you," reassured the doctor. "Except for the arrival of all these flowers, you didn't miss a thing."

"Who sent them?"

"Let's see, the roses are from your boss and the rest of them are from KMBR listeners, I think." He slanted her a smile. "You've got a lot of fans out there—I happen to be one of them."

"Really?"

"Oh, yeah," he said. "In fact, I almost think I know you,

I've become so used to hearing your voice on the radio. You do a great job, by the way."

"Well, thank you," said Erica, pleased by his words. Then she added, "How thoughtful of people to send these flowers." Distractedly, she again touched the bandages on her head. "I suppose the crash made the news."

Dr. Moncrieffe let go of Erica's hand to gesture broadly.

"Oh, it made the news, all right," he said. "People listened to the whole thing broadcast live as you dropped from the sky. I heard it myself. It was pretty dramatic."

There was a long silence as Erica tried to remember those last couple of minutes in the air. Why was it so difficult? *Think*, she told herself.

"Oh, no," she said softly, as a few images flickered in her mind, "my mike was still on, wasn't it?"

"I'm afraid so." A teasing twinkle entered his eyes. "What some people won't do to increase their listening audience."

In response, Erica felt the hint of a smile on her lips, then she said, "I can't begin to tell you how surprised I was to wake up in this beautiful place." She looked around, determined to focus on the here and now as a way of banishing the frightening images that were passing through her memory. "It certainly isn't like any hospital room I've ever seen before."

"Well, it's one of our fancier models," he said. "I felt you deserved it after your swan dive into the lake."

Erica felt warmed by his words. She knew that he was speaking as a doctor to his patient, yet she detected a flicker of interest that went beyond that. With a flash of insight, she realized that Grayson Moncrieffe truly liked and appreciated the opposite sex.

She regarded the handsome doctor more closely, for to gaze up at him momentarily took the edge off her worries, and he definitely piqued her curiosity. She could easily imagine that women liked him equally well in return. Somehow his looks and bearing didn't fit the stereotype of a physician. Why was there the air of an outlaw or rebel about him? pondered Erica.

Mentally she exchanged his surgeon's garb for jeans and a plaid shirt, and the image of a rugged outdoorsman or maverick cowboy clicked neatly into place. His broad brow and strong jawline inspired confidence; he could obviously hold his own in any situation. She liked his name, too. Did his friends call him Gray, for short? she wondered.

She ended her musings with the conclusion that Gray was the sort of man who drew women as powerfully as the moon compels the tides. His outlaw aura, with its spicy hint of rugged independence, only served to enhance his undeniable appeal.

"So . . . how long do you think I'll be here?" asked Erica, shifting on the bed and feeling every muscle in her body give an aching protest.

"It depends," said Gray, "but I think you can count on about a week."

"A week," said Erica slowly, disgesting this new bit of information.

Actually, she was glad to hear it, for, at that point, returning to her normal routine sounded more than a little daunting. After such a traumatic experience as hers, would she be able to cope with the everyday tasks of living? As she lay there thinking, a ripple of anger quickly passed through her. *Why did this have to happen to me*, she thought, *why me*?

"You're probably wondering if the station has found you a temporary replacement," commented Gray, perhaps misreading the expression on Erica's face. "It has."

"I see," she said slowly, still trying to sort things out in her befogged mind.

"So," continued Gray, giving a nod, "you'll be staying put for now."

"A week," repeated Erica. "That sounds like a long time, but I suppose it's for the best. I mean . . . I can't even imagine going back right now to such mundane things as housework, or driving my car, or going to the bank, or . . ." She felt her lips quiver and had to swallow back some tears. Then she added in a small voice, "I wonder if my life will ever be the same again."

Gray studied her for a long moment, his gaze level and assessing.

"You've had a terrible experience," he said kindly, "and you need a few days to let all of this sink in. Just take it one day at a time—there's no need to rush back to your regular routine. Be gentle with yourself—these things don't sort themselves out overnight." There was a pause, and then he chuckled, obviously trying to cheer her up. "Don't worry, you'll be up and back to normal before you know it."

"I hope you're right," she said, smiling gratefully at his attempt to buoy her spirits, but still feeling a myriad of doubts. Perhaps, for now, she would simply have to take it on faith that everything was eventually going to work out.

"What an experience," she went on. "This is the worst thing that's ever happened to me. I must still be in a state of shock."

"That's only natural," said Gray, "but you'll eventually put it all into perspective." There was a pause. "Tell me something," he went on, shifting his weight and crossing his arms over his broad chest. "What's it like to look down on traffic jams day after day? I can't imagine having that kind of job."

"I enjoy it," said Erica, glad to have the conversation take a different direction. "It gives me a lot of satisfaction."

"Satisfaction?" He looked skeptical.

"Of course," she said. "It pleases me to know that I'm helping people get back and forth to work safely."

"Hmm," said Gray, then added, half to himself, "poor old Puget Sound."

"I beg your pardon?"

A cool twinge of apprehension rippled down Erica's spine. What did Gray mean by his cryptic remark?

"Oh, I was just thinking about what it used to be like around here," said Gray, "before Seattle became so popular. Word got out about our scenic beauty, and now everyone and his brother wants to live here. Those of us who were born and raised in Seattle remember what it was like before the population explosion. We never used to have gridlocked freeways and rush hours that lasted half the day. When I was growing up, traffic reports weren't even necessary. I miss that small-town feeling."

Gray's comments made Erica feel uncomfortable. The subject of Seattle's exploding population obviously raised his hackles, but, as a newcomer herself, Erica felt stung by his words and wished that he hadn't brought up the topic. He apparently assumed that she, too, was a Washington native, or he wouldn't have launched into his candid remarks. Either that or he needed to brush up on his social-diplomacy skills.

Gazing up at his unsmiling face, Erica suddenly felt defensive. She didn't like the feeling at all. She also didn't particularly care for Gray's tone. Was he always that blunt and opinionated? she wondered. For a moment, she had the perverse desire to topple him from his soapbox by revealing that she herself was a recent transplant. Then she thought better of it. Suppressing the temptation, she decided that what their conversation needed, instead, was a light touch.

"I think fewer people would move here," she observed mildly, "if they knew how much it rains. Oh, and don't forget the squads of ravenous slugs that can turn your garden into a stump farm in a single night."

Her ploy worked.

"You're right," said Gray, nodding his head with a wry chuckle. "Instead of calling Seattle 'The Emerald City', we should've nicknamed it 'The Slug Capital of the World'."

Their shared laughter cleared the air.

"Well," said Erica presently, as she gave her hospital bed a meaningful pat, "it looks as though I'll be catching up on my reading, doesn't it?" She soberly regarded Gray. "I like your advice about taking it one day at a time. A week or so from now, this nightmare will be behind me—I hope—and I'll be back in the air."

Gray shot her a surprised glance. "Back in the air?" he said.

"Why, yes," she said, puzzled by the note of incredulity in his voice. "Of course."

"How can you even consider climbing back into a chopper after what's happened to you?" he said, shaking his head in wonderment.

"I love flying," said Erica, in a simple statement of fact.

"Well, but . . ." said Gray, his voice trailing off.

"But what?" asked Erica, experiencing a sense of uneasiness.

"I'm just thinking," said Gray, giving a little shrug, "that next time, you might not be so lucky, that's all."

"I'm not even going to worry about there being a next time," said Erica, a tone of determination in her voice.

"Hmm, I see," commented Gray, frowning slightly as he regarded her. Clearly, he thought she was quite out of her mind.

"Flying is my life—it's my passion," said Erica, suddenly feeling the need to explain herself. "There's no way I'm going to give it up and spend the rest of my days behind a desk."

"You like traffic reporting that much, then," said Gray. It was a statement, not a question.

"Whether or not I work as a reporter is not the point," said Erica. "It's the *flying* I'm talking about. Traffic reporting, taking aerial photographs, carrying passengers or freight—I'd be happy at any of those jobs as long as it involved flying. I belong up in the air, don't you see?"

"I guess not," admitted Gray, with an expressive roll of his shoulders. "Yours is an attitude I just don't identify with. I mean, think about it: You almost get killed in a helicopter crash, and then you act like you can hardly wait to climb back into one of those flimsy-looking contraptions." He paused, a thoughtful look on his face. "No offense, but if it were me, I'd call your accident a message from the gods to stay out of helicopters."

"That's ridiculous," said Erica, pooh-poohing such a notion. "And why all this interest in whether or not I fly again?" she went on, hearing a little edge in her voice. "Why should it matter to you one way or the other?"

"I'm a doctor, Ms. Johansen," said Gray, "which makes me professionally committed to maintaining your health." He regarded her, not unkindly. "Part of my job is to give advice about a patient's future behavior and well-being."

"Well, thank you, Doctor," said Erica, "but I've worked hard to get where I am today and nothing—not even falling out of the sky—is going to stop me now." Feeling her lips again trembling with emotion, she hastened on while she could still control her feelings. "You see, my parents died when I was just a kid, and I was raised by my aunt, who had no money to send me to college. I had to do all of that on my own. I've paid my dues, Dr. Moncrieffe." She emphasized her point by hitting the bed with her fist.

"And even though I have no regrets," she went on in an impassioned tone, "I can never forget that I had to scrape and hustle to make it through school and get my degree and my pilot's license. Flying has been my goal ever since I was a child. I've spent all of my adult life preparing for a career in aviation, and I intend to hang on to my dream with both hands. Accidents happen, Doctor, but life goes on." She paused to catch her breath, then she added, "As I said, in a few days I'll be back in the air. I didn't come all the way out here from Denver to give up when the going got tough."

"You're from Denver?" said Gray, looking at her sharply.

"Yes," said Erica, chiding herself for her slip of the tongue. "I've lived here for about a year. I wasn't going to tell you, because you obviously have strong feelings about 'outsiders'."

"So you came out here when you were offered the job at KMBR?"

"That's right," said Erica. "I was willing to move any-where on the planet, as long as the job involved flying." She gave a little smile. "It just happened to be Seattle, that's all."

"I see," said Gray, studying her. "Well, now that you're here, I hope you're enjoying the outdoor lifestyle that the Northwest is so famous for." He paused. "Are you into skiing or backpacking?"

"Not really," said Erica, with a brief laugh. "I've never been what you'd call the outdoorsy type. Skiing doesn't really interest me and I've never been on a hike in my life."

"Hmm," said Gray, a thoughtful look on his handsome face. Then he shifted his weight and added, "That was some speech you gave about working hard to get where you are. You're pretty feisty." His eyes twinkled down at her. "I'd hate to tangle with you when you're fully recovered and on your feet.

"I must admit, though," he went on smoothly, "that spir-ited women are much more interesting than pushovers. My compliments." He dipped his head in a brief salute that expressed a sense of playfulness, not rancor.

Before Erica could react to this change of pace, which was both intriguing and unexpected, Gray went right on.

"I probably owe you an apology," he said, with disarming sincerity. "I shouldn't have ranted about Seattle's population explosion, especially without knowing whether or not you were from here yourself. Please don't take anything I said as a personal attack." A wan smile crossed his lips. "I was merely lamenting for a way of life that's gone forever."

"It's all right," said Erica, tentatively returning his smile.

Gray gazed at her with good humor emanating from the twin pools of his eyes.

Oh, those intoxicating eyes. Now, instead of impaling her with unwavering intensity, as they had done during their brief discussion of flying, they roamed over her face and hair with frank interest. She felt a sudden rush of heat as a pleasant tingling sensation raced along her spine. Under different circumstances, Erica would've sworn that Gray was flirting with her. Just then she remembered something.

"Say, you haven't told me what happened right after the crash," she said, feeling a weight again descending on her emotions. "How on earth did I get out of the helicopter? I don't recall a thing after receiving that thump on the head."

"Yes, I suppose you are a bit curious about all that," said Gray. "Well, as I told you, I was listening to KMBR when your traffic report came on. When I saw that the chopper was in trouble, I—"

"Wait a minute," broke in Erica. "You *saw* us going down?"

"That's right. You see, I happened to be in the area and—"

At that moment, Gray's pager beeped, halting his narrative. He tossed Erica an apologetic look.

"Sorry for the interruption," he said, reaching for the sleek lavender telephone beside her bed. He punched in a number, his features set in concentration. "Gray Moncrieffe here." His tone was brisk and professional.

Erica, who found herself covertly watching him, was again struck by his demeanor. Gray could obviously be outspoken and a little too generous with his opinions, but Erica grudgingly had to admit that he no doubt meant well and that he inspired confidence. It was also clear that he was used to giving orders and having others defer to him.

"We may have to increase the dosage," said Gray into the telephone. "I'd better check him myself, nurse. I'll be right there." He was about to hang up, then added, "Oh, nurse, if my attorney calls, please tell him I need to talk with him later this afternoon about the Wagner House. Yes, that's right. Thanks." With that, he hung up the receiver and looked down at Erica.

"Duty calls," he said. "I have to leave—sorry."

Erica regarded him, her mind having suddenly veered off in an entirely unexpected direction. Had she heard Gray correctly, or was her still-befuddled mind playing tricks on her? She had to ask.

"Excuse me for prying," she said, "but did you just mention the Wagner House?"

"Yes," said Gray, "you know the place?"

"You might say that," said Erica, choosing her words carefully. "I'm on the Board of Antiquities."

There was a long silence as Gray appeared to mentally assess her disclosure.

"Well, well," he finally said, "what a small world."

"What do you mean?" asked Erica.

"I'm the person who's trying to buy that place," said Gray, "and have it torn down."

"You?" said Erica, scarcely believing her ears.

"That's right," said Gray briskly, "and you're exactly the person I want to talk to about that—when you're feeling better, of course."

"What's there to talk about?" said Erica, feeling a tide of battle rising in her. "You already know where the Board stands on the issue."

"Yes, of course I do," said Gray. "They've put up some legal roadblocks that are holding up the sale, for now. But," he added meaningfully, "if I can convince just one member of the Board to see things my way, that person can persuade the others."

"And you think that I am that person?" said Erica, gazing back at him in cool disbelief.

"Quite possibly," said Gray. "I'm sure you'll agree with me, once I've explained my plan for that property."

"You'll never change my mind," said Erica. "You'd be wasting your breath."

"Well, we'll see," said Gray.

His tone of voice was so laced with self-assurance that Erica longed to hurl some none-too-complimentary remarks in his direction.

"Wait," she called out to him instead, for he was preparing to leave. "You never told me how I got here."

"I'll stop by this evening and finish the story," he responded. "In the meantime, get some rest and try not to worry. You're going to be okay."

"Try not to worry," muttered Erica under her breath. "Easy for you to say."

Then she chided herself for her impatience. The man was just trying to reassure her—it was part of his job, after all. But then she remembered their uncomfortable little exchange about the dangers of flying, topped off by the unwelcome discovery that Gray was behind the plan to destroy the Wagner House, and it all seemed too overwhelming.

Feeling suddenly drained of her energy, she sank back on her pillow. Closing her eyes, she willed her brain to shut down for a while and let her escape from the waking world and its troubles.

She spent the rest of the afternoon drifting in and out of sleep. Her body ached all over, as if she'd been pummeled by sandbags. Efficient, soft-spoken nurses came and went, seeing to her every need. Her IV was removed and she sat up briefly to eat a meal consisting of soft, easily digested foods. Afterward, she lay down again, feeling somewhat revived.

Later on, she telephoned Buzz, who was in a room down the hall. The pilot was still a bit woozy but in good spirits, and made Erica laugh several times by joking about their plunge into the lake. Even so, Erica felt tears coursing down her cheeks as she spoke with Buzz, brought on by a mixture of emotions: enormous gratitude that she and Buzz had been spared, unnamed fears about the future, and a gnawing sense of loss and confusion with regard to the days that she had lain unconscious.

Hanging up the receiver, Erica glanced over at the balcony doors through the veil of moisture that clouded her vision. The shadows of early evening were beginning to lengthen among the ferns and other plantings. Again weariness tugged at her mind. She wiped away her tears, blew her nose, and struggled to keep her eyes open, for she wanted to be composed and awake when Dr. Moncrieffe returned. Although she keenly felt the awkwardness caused by their opposing views over the fate of the Wagner House, she was nevertheless burning to know exactly how she'd been freed from the sinking chopper. On that subject, she could hardly wait to speak with the doctor.

Before long, however, her feelings of sleepiness overpowered her resolve to stay awake, and she felt herself drifting off. Sighing deeply, she finally yielded to the delicious sensation that was enveloping her. Sleep enfolded her like a soft cashmere cloak, and she sank into a healing dreamlessness.

Lovely golden rays from the summer sun flooded Erica's room the next morning as a young nurse opened the drapes. Erica yawned and stretched, noting with satisfaction that some of the soreness had left her body.

"Mmm," she murmured, "good morning."

"Good morning, Ms. Johansen," said the nurse.

She bustled over to Erica's bed and raised the top half of it so that Erica could sit up. Erica saw by a plastic tag on the nurse's lapel that her name was Leslie.

"Feeling better today?" inquired Leslie, plumping pillows.

"Yes," said Erica, "but I was so out of it yesterday, I

forgot to ask what hospital this is. Where am I, anyway?"

"You're on the fourth floor of the Moncrieffe Medical Center."

"Oh," said Erica, "no wonder it's so elegant. I've heard about this place." It was right around the corner from the old Wagner house, for one thing. There was a short pause as Erica thought of something else.

"Hmm," she said, "what a coincidence."

The nurse was preparing to take Erica's temperature. She hesitated, halting the progress of the thermometer to within a few inches of Erica's lips.

"Oh?" said Leslie. "What do you mean?"

"My doctor has the same name as this hospital," said Erica, and opened her mouth for the advancing thermometer.

"That's not a coincidence," said Leslie, with a laugh. She lowered the instrument and gave Erica an amused look. "Dr. Moncrieffe's grandfather founded the Center—in 1920, I believe. Dr. Moncrieffe's father runs the hospital now, and Gray and his cousin Richard—he's a physician, too—work here."

Erica's mouth closed as the nurse's words sank in. She'd heard a lot about the world-famous Moncrieffe Medical Center. It impressed her that a member of the powerful and prestigious Moncrieffe family had been taking care of her.

"Was Dr. Moncrieffe in to see me last night?" she asked.

"Yes, but you were sound asleep by then."

"I hope he'll drop by this morning."

"I'm afraid not today."

"Oh?" Erica felt an unexpected twinge of disappointment. "Why not?"

"He'll be out of town for a few days," explained Leslie. "I think he's speaking at a conference in Atlanta."

"Darn," said Erica with a sigh. "He promised to tell me how I got out of the helicopter after it crashed." She shook her head. "I have absolutely no idea what happened."

"Oh, my goodness," said Leslie, "I just assumed that he'd explained everything to you yesterday."

Something in the nurse's tone fanned Erica's curiosity even more.

"No, he didn't get a chance to," she said. "Please tell me about it."

Leslie again raised the thermometer. The instrument hovered near Erica's lips.

"Ms. Johansen," said the nurse, "Dr. Moncrieffe himself pulled you from that wreck." She paused for dramatic effect. "Why, he saved your life."

Chapter Three

"**M**mph!"

Erica's exclamation of surprise was cut short as the nurse took advantage of her patient's open mouth and slipped the thermometer between her lips. Leslie directed her to close down on the instrument, and Erica obediently did as she was told.

Waiting restlessly, Erica almost tapped her fingers on the blanket, she was so eager to hear more. Her mind whirled with questions as she stared up at Leslie. After what seemed like an eternity, the nurse finally removed the thermometer from Erica's mouth and reached for her chart.

"Nurse," said Erica, leaning forward, "please tell me what happened. Dr. Moncrieffe saved my life? How?"

"He was sailing his boat on Lake Washington that morning," began Leslie, looking up from her notations.

"There were lots of sailboats that day," broke in Erica,

31

thinking back. "I remember one, in particular. We came very close to it as we headed for the water."

"It was probably Dr. Moncrieffe's."

The jumbled images were returning to Erica in wave after wave, unfolding in slow motion and allowing her to see details that she'd only half registered at the time.

"There was a man on the boat," she said, her eyes staring into the middle distance. "He . . . he had on a blue sweater." She hesitated, concentrating on the blurred visions that were beginning to come into focus in her mind.

"And he had a mustache," she said, with mounting excitement. She looked at Leslie. "The man on the boat had a mustache! No wonder Dr. Moncrieffe looked so familiar to me. He was the man on the sailboat." She lay back, suddenly tired from the effort of remembering.

"You know," she continued more calmly, "it all happened so fast. I only got a quick look at him, but I can see him now so clearly in my mind. He was staring up at the chopper and shading his eyes against the sun. He probably felt as helpless as we did, but there was nothing he could do but watch us go down.

"Actually," she went on, giving Leslie a wan smile, "I've had several dreams about the crash since then."

"That's to be expected," said Leslie. "You must feel so lucky to be alive."

"You can say that again," said Erica, with quiet emphasis. After a reflective pause, she eagerly returned to the story, asking, "Then what happened, after we actually hit the water?"

"Dr. Moncrieffe swam over to your helicopter," said Leslie, "dove under the water, and somehow pulled you and your pilot out. You were unconscious by that time."

"That sounds very dangerous," said Erica, with a little shiver. "Why, he could've been pulled down with us."

Leslie shrugged. "You know, I don't think it would even occur to him to be afraid." She snapped her fingers. "He'd just do whatever needed to be done."

Erica silently concurred with the nurse's assessment. Gray Moncrieffe had struck her from the first as a man who would naturally step in and take charge. It was hard not to admire a man like that.

"Besides," continued Leslie, "he's in terrific shape and must be a strong swimmer. He's always off on some wilderness adventure, so he has to be very fit."

"He likes to travel, does he?" asked Erica, feeling a surge of interest that surprised her.

An image of Gray's handsome face came sharply into view in her mind's eye. A shimmering aura of courage and romantic derring-do surrounded the vision. The attractive physician suddenly seemed fascinating—and a little mysterious—to Erica.

"Oh, yes," said Leslie, answering Erica's question. "He's been all over the world and done some incredible things, like floating the Amazon River in a kayak and trekking all over Nepal. But he says that his favorite place is Alaska." She smiled at Erica and tucked in a corner of the bed. "Some of his travel pictures are hanging out in the hall. They're really beautiful, especially the ones of wild animals."

"I'll look forward to seeing them," said Erica, with a preoccupied air. Then she returned to their original topic. "What happened after we were pulled out of the lake?"

"You and your pilot were rushed here by ambulance," said Leslie, "and Dr. Moncrieffe insisted that you be given this room."

Erica glanced around. The Moncrieffe Medical Center certainly was a comfortable place in which to recuperate. Besides that, it was always in the news about something, she reflected. Either a famous person had checked in for some delicate surgery, or there'd been another medical breakthrough in the Center's research unit.

For a moment, Erica imagined that she could feel the power and prestige of that great institution vibrating around her. It was humbling to know that a grandson of the founder had rescued her from certain death. Once again, she was struck with amazement that Gray had placed himself in danger in order to save her and Buzz.

Then, before she could stop herself, Erica began voicing a question that had been unaccountably teasing around the edges of her mind.

"I wonder . . ."

"Yes?" said Leslie.

"I wonder if Dr. Moncrieffe's wife was upset when she found out that her husband had risked his life to save ours."

"Oh, there's no Mrs. Moncrieffe," replied the nurse briskly. "I think he was engaged a few years back, but it apparently didn't work out. In any case, he's unattached."

Erica could tell that Leslie enjoyed a bit of gossip. Shamelessly, she let her prattle on.

"Which is a pity, really," the nurse continued, with a knowing air. "I mean, he's such a wonderful man—and very attractive, as you must've noticed. I'm sure he has no trouble getting dates, and someday he'll make some lucky woman his wife."

Why Erica should take any interest in such personal details about a man she barely knew was unclear to her. Still, there was no denying that she was interested. Leslie broke in on her thoughts.

"He's very dedicated to helping others, you know," she said. "Why, he sat right in that chair the entire first night you were here."

"He did?" said Erica, after a longish pause.

"Yes," said Leslie, "and he brought you those flowers, too." She gestured toward the blue irises in the Chinese vase.

Erica looked over at the bouquet, her favorite of all the floral arrangements that had been sent to cheer her. On long, graceful stalks, the blooms had opened a bit more since the previous day. In their centers, Erica could see a smudge of gold. The way their petals curled outward reminded her of delicately poised butterflies on the first glorious day of summer.

Well, well. So Gray Moncrieffe had sat up with her during her first night in the hospital, and had provided elegant flowers to brighten her stay. Leslie was right—he was very dedicated. His attentiveness toward Erica was probably even more pronounced because he'd saved her life.

Leslie started bustling around, gathering up her things to leave.

"Would you happen to have any newspaper articles about the crash?" asked Erica. "I'd really like to learn more about it."

"Let me check the staff lounge," said Leslie, and left the room.

A few minutes later, she reappeared with a back issue of *The Seattle Times* and placed it in Erica's eager hands.

"Thanks," said Erica.

Leslie continued on her rounds and Erica settled back to read. She found that the article about the traffic chopper's dramatic plummet from the sky took up most of the front page. It was accompanied by still shots from an amateur videotape that someone had taken from one of the stalled vehicles on the bridge.

Erica's throat constricted with horror as she studied the pictures: One of the chopper pointing nose-down toward the water, another of it entering the lake with an enormous splash, and then—most terrible of all—a swath of floating debris.

Erica dragged her eyes away from the surreal and haunting images—a catastrophic event frozen in time, frame by frame—and skimmed the text. The information in it meshed with Leslie's version of the story: Gray Moncrieffe had indeed saved Erica's life. It was such an astonishing revelation that it was hard to digest all at once.

Finally putting the paper aside, one thought dominated all others in Erica's mind: She owed Dr. Moncrieffe a huge debt of gratitude. Life was precious to her, and it was no small thing to have been snatched from the cold, uncaring hands of death.

She caught her breath, squeezed her eyes shut, and tears began to flow as the enormity of the accident hit home. She and Buzz had been in that falling chopper, they had sustained the impact of it smashing into the lake, then they had been beneath that floating patch of debris, sinking toward their death in the murky waters that were, by then, pouring into the cockpit. Erica's sobs filled the room for several long minutes, a keening sound that expressed helpless horror at what had happened to her, interspersed with stammered prayers of gratitude.

As her emotions gradually settled down, Erica felt drained but reassured and a peaceful calmness stole over her. She would never, ever take life for granted again. She had been spared. With trembling hands, she reached for some tissues to dry her face. The cleansing power of tears had cleared both her eyes and her thinking. She had been in a terrible accident, but she now believed, deep in her soul, that everything was going to be all right.

Several minutes went by as Erica mulled over her insights and composed herself, then she reached for the telephone. She must contact Dr. Moncrieffe right away and thank him. She stared at the instrument for a moment, then lay back against the pillows as she remembered that Gray was out of town and wouldn't return for several days.

She expelled her breath as some mixed feelings passed through her. Certainly, she wanted to thank Gray for his bravery. Plus, he'd brought her flowers and sat up with her that first night. If she hadn't already formed a different opinion of him, she'd have said that the man was a saint.

But Gray was no saint, a fact he'd proven during their first encounter. He was too free with his opinions and advice and—what a surprising disclosure—he was at the heart of the Wagner House controversy. On balance, Erica didn't much like the man.

Another point to consider was that of obligation. Having

always paid her own way in life, Erica didn't enjoy being in someone's debt, especially not to someone like Gray. She sighed, for the antagonism she felt toward him made things very awkward. Still, the task of thanking him for saving her life had to be faced and she would do just that.

Erica plucked at her blanket in frustration. She disliked having to put things off, especially unwelcome tasks. A face-to-face acknowledgement of her debt to Gray was a scene she wanted behind her—and soon. It would be hard to wait for his return from Atlanta, but clearly she had no other choice.

Chapter Four

Afew days later, Erica was sitting on the edge of her bed, dressed and ready to leave the Moncrieffe Medical Center. It was a lovely morning to be released from the hospital, she mused, admiring the summer light that was streaming through the balcony doors.

Even though her stay had been more pleasant than the usual hospital confinement, she was eager to return to her own home, a houseboat on Seattle's Lake Union, and resume her normal routine. She would even have gone straight back to work if Marty, her boss, hadn't stopped by and insisted that she take some extra days off.

Erica glanced at her watch and felt a ripple of nervousness. Gray Moncrieffe would be there in a few minutes. He'd been out of town since their first encounter, but he'd left a message that morning that he was back and would stop in to see her before her release. Nurse Leslie had mentioned, too, that Gray had called several times during his absence, to check on Erica's progress.

Erica looked over at the blue irises that Gray had given her. Now past their prime, the faded long-stemmed beauties nevertheless still looked elegant in their lovely vase. Erica had arranged to have the vase sent to her houseboat as the only item she was saving from the floral gifts that had arrived after her accident. She knew that every time she looked at the vase in the future, she'd be reminded of Dr. Moncrieffe's extraordinary act of courage.

Just then, an image of Gray's face appeared in Erica's mind. The man had saved her life. Her stomach fluttered as she considered what she'd say to him to express her gratitude. Words seemed so inadequate.

She fought the impulse to look at her watch again. Instead, she stood up and walked out onto the balcony to gaze at the quiet, park-like grounds below, with snow-capped Mount Rainier hovering in the distance. She took a deep breath and tried to calm herself, but her jitters persisted.

Catching her reflection in the sliding glass door, she distracted herself by smoothing imaginary creases from her slacks and adjusting the open collar of her tailored shirt. She'd captured her blond hair with a wide clip at the nape of her neck, and was wearing some simple gold earrings she'd bought in Norway. She'd fussed over her appearance a bit more than usual that morning, in self-conscious preparation for her meeting with Gray.

Hearing someone enter the room, Erica turned to see Dr. Grayson Moncrieffe striding toward her. Her stomach flip-flopped and her breath caught in her throat. She'd never felt that nervous in her life.

"Good morning," said Gray, joining her on the balcony. "How're you feeling?"

Erica looked up into his intensely brown eyes and felt a momentary lightheadedness, as if she were a little tipsy. Out there in the sunshine, she could see that Gray's dark hair and mustache were shot with rich highlights of red and gold, in addition to the few threads of silver that she'd noticed before.

Distractedly, she wondered what it would be like to sift her fingers through Gray's hair, or to feel his mustache brush against her lips. Her heart pulsed as she chided herself for having such thoughts.

Today Gray's hair was neatly combed, in contrast with their last meeting, when he'd appeared tousled and in need of sleep. For a moment, Erica felt a pang of guilt as she reflected that his sitting up with her during those first terrible hours after the crash had probably caused him additional fatigue.

"Hello," she said, "I'm feeling much better, thank you." She laughed briefly. "As nice as this place is, I'm really looking forward to going home."

"Yes," said Gray, "I can imagine that."

His wide, attractive mouth curved into a smile, and Erica noticed how his eyes lit up. His skin glowed with good health, and he exuded the kind of raw animal vitality that Erica had encountered before in people who were physically fit and who led adventuresome lifestyles.

As they stood in the warm sunshine, Erica noted another change from their first meeting. Now, instead of surgical scrubs, Gray was dressed in casual street clothes. His classic white shirt was open at the neck, his long legs were sheathed in tailored slacks, and his soft leather loafers were polished and expensive-looking.

Over his shirt, he wore a Harris tweed sports jacket that fit his broad shoulders to a T, its elegant, unself-conscious appearance suggesting that it might be his favorite article of clothing. Today Gray could easily pass for a country gentleman from an English estate, mused Erica, except for the stethoscope that she could see poking out from one of his jacket pockets.

Gray was studying her closely. "You look very well," he said. "I'm happy to see some color back in your cheeks. You were so pale the last time we talked."

Erica cleared her throat and tried to remember the little speech that she'd prepared.

"Dr. Moncrieffe, I—" she began.

"Let's not be so formal," he smoothly interjected. "Please call me Gray. May I call you Erica?"

Erica had the impression that Gray was trying to put her at her ease. His eyes were certainly perceptive, and he could no doubt sense how nervous she was. Slowly she let out her breath. Perhaps this meeting wasn't going to be as difficult as she'd imagined.

"Yes, of course," she said, agreeing to a first-name basis. She tried again. "Gray, I really want to thank you for saving my life."

He looked off into the distance for a moment, his expression unreadable. Then he returned his gaze to Erica and briefly lifted his shoulders in a gesture of nonchalance.

"Well, you know what they say," he commented. "I happened to be in the right place at the right time." His tone was studiedly off-hand.

Erica wondered why Gray was playing down his part in her rescue. He didn't seem the type who'd assume a facade of false modesty. Then it occurred to her that his act of bravery was probably not extraordinary for a man with his experience and background.

Still, it wasn't everyone who would risk his own life in order to save two people who were sinking underwater in a helicopter. She voiced her feelings.

"What you did for Buzz and me was amazing and exceptional," she said, then noticed a look of uneasiness in his eyes and some tension in his jaw. "Have I said something to offend you?" she asked.

"No, it's nothing you've said," he responded, gesturing with one hand. "Sorry if I sound brusque. I was just thinking about what a circus it was after I pulled you out."

"What do you mean?"

"I wish the newspapers hadn't splashed the details all over the front page," he said, with a rueful expression. "I hate being in the limelight." His eyes narrowed with remembered annoyance.

"Then the wire services got wind of the story," he went on, "and I was contacted by one of those tabloid TV shows, hounding me for an interview." He raised his brows in an expression of ill-concealed disapproval of such entertainment venues. "Naturally, I turned them down flat. I'm afraid I wasn't very nice about it, either, but the guy who kept calling me just wouldn't take no for an answer."

"I'm sorry you were exposed to all that," said Erica, not knowing what else to say, but feeling somehow responsible.

"Oh, forget it," said Gray, the hardness in his features softening. "It certainly wasn't your fault. I guess it's just human nature to focus on something dramatic like that and then blow it all out of proportion."

"Everyone likes a hero," observed Erica.

"Yeah, I guess," said Gray, dismissing the subject.

Erica hesitated, moistening her lips. She'd been rehearsing what she wanted to say to Gray and she was determined to express her gratitude, even though he was not in an especially receptive mood. She swallowed and pressed on.

"You may be able to shrug off what you did," she said, "but I can't. You saved my life, the most precious thing I have. I owe you a tremendous debt. Saying thanks just doesn't seem like enough. Plus, there's this lovely room, and those beautiful irises that you sent . . ." She blinked, forcing back the emotions that were threatening to spill over.

There was an awkward pause. Then Gray, who'd been looking deeply into Erica's eyes, seemed to will himself to relax. He reached out and gave her shoulder a squeeze. Through the thin fabric of her shirt, Erica felt the shape and strength of Gray's fingers imprinting themselves on her skin. Rivers of warmth flowed through her veins like a healing balm.

"You owe me nothing," said Gray. "Your thanks are more than enough." His deep voice vibrated in Erica's ears. "You've expressed yourself eloquently," he added, "and I appreciate that."

Then he broke contact with her shoulder and said, "You know, I can't help but think that the KMBR listeners are the luckiest ones in this whole situation." He slipped his hands into his pockets and assumed a casual stance. "You're an excellent reporter, Erica. As you know, I'm a regular listener and one of your biggest fans, so—" he smiled—"I believe I can speak with some authority on the subject. If you hadn't survived, it would've been a real loss to the Northwest."

"Does that mean you've forgiven me for being a transplant?" teased Erica.

"Ouch," said Gray, pretending to wince. "Did you have to remind me of my attack of foot-in-mouth disease?"

Erica laughed along with him, the unshed tears now gone from her eyes. She suspected, though, that Gray had purposely steered the conversation away from his role in Erica's rescue. The subject definitely made him uncomfortable and she wondered why. Her instincts told her that there was more to his aversion than irritation over unwanted publicity. Gray broke in on her speculation.

"So, what are your plans, if you don't mind my asking?" he said. "Are you going back to your traffic-reporting job, or have you thought over what I said about flying and opted for a desk assignment, instead?" He cocked an eyebrow at her. "As if I don't already know the answer to that question, right?"

"Right," said Erica in dry understatement. "I'm definitely going back to my regular job. I love flying, remember?"

"Yeah, I remember," said Gray, then added, "You're crazy, you know that?" Although he spoke in a semi-kidding tone, there was a serious edge to his voice.

"Maybe," said Erica, unflinchingly returning his gaze. Pursuing another tack, she said, "Does all of this free advice of yours have anything to do with a secret belief that women shouldn't have high-risk jobs?"

"Of course not," said Gray. "I'm merely concerned about your future safety. Give me some credit."

"You're not making that very easy," Erica tossed right back at him.

A few tense seconds ticked by. Finally Gray ended the silence.

"Well, I suppose you're lucky to be doing something that you like so much," he said, with an air of reluctantly yielding her the point about flying.

"That's something you should understand," said Erica, gladly shifting away from their conflict. "You seem to love what you're doing, too—being a doctor, I mean."

"Yes, I do," he said sincerely.

Their conversation was cut short just then as a nurse entered the room. She was pushing an empty wheelchair.

"It's time to go, Ms. Johansen, if you're ready," said the nurse. "Your cab's waiting at the main entrance."

Erica and Gray left the balcony. Gray picked up Erica's small suitcase, which Marty's wife had thoughtfully packed and brought to the hospital a couple of days earlier. Then the two of them approached the wheelchair.

"Do I have to ride in this thing?" said Erica, giving a little grimace. "I'd feel kind of silly being pushed around when I'm perfectly okay."

"It's hospital policy," said the nurse, with an understanding smile.

"We can waive policy," said Gray to Erica, "if you really think you can make it on your own."

"Great," breathed Erica.

"It's all right, nurse," said Gray. "I'll take responsibility and escort Ms. Johansen to her cab myself. We won't need this."

"Very well, Dr. Moncrieffe," said the nurse, and left the room with the wheelchair.

"Thanks," said Erica.

"You're welcome," said Gray, smiling. "It helps to have a little clout around here." He paused. "There's only one condition."

"What's that?"

Her pulse fluttered at Gray's nearness. She caught a subtle whiff of musky men's cologne. Hmm . . . very sexy.

"I'll let you walk out of here on your own power," he said, "but you've got to hang on to my arm."

He was keeping his tone light, but Erica could hear the note of concern just below the surface.

"It's a deal," she said.

She took his arm, which he was holding out for her. Beneath the nubby wool sleeve, Erica could feel Gray's strength. His arm felt like a sturdy column of oak. A warm sensation of being safe and protected rippled through Erica as Gray escorted her from the room.

They began to walk down the hall toward the elevator. When they came to Gray's travel photographs, Erica drew attention to them.

"Your pictures are really wonderful," she said. "I saw them the other day when I visited Buzz."

"Thanks." His expression quickened. "I love being out in nature, taking pictures of animals and wild country. Just give me ten minutes to pack and I'll be ready to go again." His enthusiasm lit up his face.

As they continued along the corridor, Erica once more admired the large color photographs lining the walls. There was a dramatic shot of Alaska grizzly bears fishing for spawning salmon in a rushing river. Another portrait showed a pride of lions drowsing in the shade on the African savanna. Still another shot featured a soaring condor silhouetted against the towering, snowcapped Andes.

When they arrived at the elevator, the doors opened in front of them and they stepped inside. The doors slid together with a little hiss, forming an impersonal blank wall that stared back at Erica.

For a second, she thought she saw the wall move toward her. She blinked a couple of times, knowing that her eyes had played a trick on her. Even so, she felt some beads of perspiration break out on her upper lip. Swallowing hard, she fought down a sudden upwelling of nausea as the elevator began moving downward. A vague feeling of dread, which she tried in vain to ignore, tightened around her chest.

"That's funny," she said, clinging to Gray's arm.

"What is?" said Gray.

"Elevators have never bothered me before," she said.

"Feeling a little claustrophobic?" he asked, studying her face. "Well, it's a short trip to the bottom. We're almost there."

A suffocating blanket of dread suddenly enshrouded Erica. She felt as if coils of panic were clasping her tighter and tighter until she couldn't breathe. The sensation of nausea was getting worse as her stomach churned with anxiety. Feeling dizzy and smothered, she gulped for air.

"What's going on?" she said, half to herself. "Why—why do I feel like this?"

Clutching Gray's arm, she sagged against him. She closed her eyes, hoping to block out the impression that the four walls were closing in on her, but that only intensified her dizziness and stomach-churning fear.

"What do you mean?" asked Gray, concern in his voice.

He reached around Erica's shoulders and supported her with a strong arm. Erica leaned against his solid form, hanging on to him as if he were a rock in a tossing ocean and she were a drowning woman. She spoke.

"The walls are . . . are closing in . . . closing in on me."

Her voice sounded small and frightened. Erica could barely hear her own words because of the ringing in her ears. Panic had her firmly in its grip now and was squeezing her like a huge predatory snake.

She pressed harder against Gray. Mixed in with her panic was the sensation of bewilderment. She'd never been afraid in an elevator before. It was terrible to feel so helpless and out of control.

"What did you say?" asked Gray. "I can hardly hear you. What is it, Erica? Tell me." He held her closer, as if trying to draw her terror away from her and into his own sturdy being.

"I'm falling . . . I'm falling . . . the walls are so close . . . I can't breathe . . . I'm going to drown."

Her voice was even fainter now. Gray leaned his head down to catch her words. Then Erica's hands flew out in front of her, clawing for a means of escape that wasn't there.

"Help me!" she cried. "Help me!"

"You're going to be all right," said Gray, comprehending at last. He put his other arm around her. "You're having a panic attack, Erica. Just hang on to me. We're almost there. Hang on, Erica."

He cradled her snugly against him, but his reassurance wasn't enough. Losing the battle, Erica felt her knees buckle beneath her. The world spun to a halt and suddenly went black as she fainted, a final cry for help frozen on her lips.

Chapter Five

Erica opened her eyes. She blinked a couple of times, trying to dispel the blurred images that still swam in her brain. As last the fog lifted and the world settled into focus again.

The first thing she saw was Gray, whose face wore a mask of concern. He was leaning over her as she lay on a settee in the hospital lobby. He'd apparently carried her out of the elevator and placed her there after she'd fainted. Onlookers hovered nearby, whispering among themselves, and Erica suddenly felt self-conscious. She struggled to sit up as the heat of a blush invaded her neck and face.

"Hey, not so fast," advised Gray. "There's no hurry. Just rest for a couple of minutes."

He gently pushed her back down onto the settee and gave her his hand, which she gratefully clung to. Then he turned toward a nurse, who was standing beside them.

"She'll be fine, nurse," he said. "Thank you."

"All right, Dr. Moncrieffe," said the woman. "If you need me, I'll be at the desk."

The nurse walked off. As if this was a signal that the excitement was over, the rest of the onlookers drifted away, leaving Gray and Erica to themselves.

"I'm so embarrassed," said Erica, smiling sheepishly. "What on earth happened back there? I've never been afraid in an elevator before."

She was baffled by her reaction. She'd always been a vigorous, healthy person, and had never before experienced anything like the episode she'd just gone through. Feeling out of control was a new sensation for her, and Erica didn't care for it one bit. She spoke again.

"What did you call it—a panic attack? I certainly don't like the sound of that," she added with dismay.

"Panic attacks can happen to anyone," explained Gray. "They aren't that uncommon, especially if a person's just been through a traumatic event the way you have."

"I think I can sit up now."

Her smile was shaky, but she was already feeling better. Gray gave her an assist, then sat down beside her. She straightened her clothing and swept a few loose strands of hair out of her face. Glancing around, she was glad to see that no one was staring at her anymore. Somewhere down the corridor a soft-spoken message was being broadcast over the public-address system, and Erica could hear the muted ringing of a telephone at the desk. Everything seemed to be back to normal, but what about her?

She turned to Gray in puzzlement. "You mean that being in the elevator somehow triggered a recurrence of the fear and panic I felt when the helicopter went down?"

"That seems the most likely explanation," said Gray, "especially if you've never had such a reaction before."

"No, never," she said, shaking her head firmly. "This has caught me completely off guard."

"You mentioned something about the walls closing in on you," said Gray, his brow furrowing.

Erica felt a twinge of discomfort at his words and she moistened her lips. She stared down at her hands, which were tightly clasped together in her lap.

"That's right," she finally responded softly. "The walls were closing in and I had the sensation of falling and of being trapped at the same time." She shuddered. "It was horrible."

Then she rubbed her forehead as an awful possibility entered her mind.

"This isn't going to be a permanent condition, is it?" she said. "I mean, is that how I'm going to feel from now on, panic-stricken and sick to my stomach whenever I'm in an elevator or some other enclosed space?" Her voice was laced with worry.

"Hey, take it easy," said Gray in a reassuring manner. "For some people, panic reactions happen once in a lifetime. For others, there may be several episodes after a trauma, but the attacks become milder until they finally disappear altogether." He hesitated. "There are some cases, of course, in which the attacks persist."

Erica swallowed. "You mean—you mean, they just keep happening every time . . . ?" Her voice trailed off into a whisper. "Oh, no . . . no." She felt her throat constrict. "I can't live like that. I have to get my life back on track again." She stared grimly into space, as if straining to see into the future.

"Can you imagine what panic attacks would do to my career?" she went on in an ironic tone. "It would be the end of flying, that's for sure."

"You may never have another attack as long as you live," said Gray matter-of-factly. "Don't jump to conclusions."

"I hope you're right," said Erica, with a bleak sigh. Then, needing to lighten her mood, she smiled at Gray. "Say, thanks for your help—again. That's twice you've rescued me." Then she abruptly sat forward. "Oh, my gosh," she exclaimed, looking toward the entrance doors. "I completely forgot about my cab."

"I tipped the cabbie and sent him on his way," said Gray, helping Erica to her feet. "I'm driving you home myself. After that scene in the elevator, I'd feel much better if I personally saw you to your doorstep. After all, it was on my okay that you skipped the wheelchair." He paused. "How do you feel?"

"Fine," she said, shrugging, and it was almost true. Her muscles still ached a little from the crash, but, except for the frightening episode on their way down to the lobby, she felt all right.

"But are you sure you can spare the time?" she asked. "I'd hate to impose on you. You've done so much for me already."

Gray picked up her suitcase and steered her out the door and toward the parking lot across the street.

"Don't worry," he told her, "I can spare the time. My shift today doesn't start until this evening. It's not an imposition and, besides," he added, flashing her a smile that was obviously intended to charm her, "I'm hoping to work a little gentle persuasion on you, remember?"

"I suppose you're referring to the Wagner House," said Erica.

"I am."

"That house is *not* coming down," said Erica firmly.

"We'll talk," said Gray, smoothly tabling the topic for the moment as he guided her between the cars.

They halted beside a sleek black Jaguar, a classic beauty from a previous decade. Gray reached in his pocket for his keys, stowed Erica's suitcase in the trunk, then opened the passenger side.

Erica felt hesitant about entering the confined space of the car. What if she had another panic attack?

Gray was studying her across the Jaguar's door, which he was holding open for her.

"You're nervous about getting in, aren't you?" he said.

Erica's palms were damp. "As a matter of fact," she admitted with a short burst of shaky laughter, "I am. How can you tell?"

"I can see it in your eyes," he said.

Erica wasn't used to being with a man who was so perceptive, and who watched her with such frank appraisal.

"You don't miss much, do you?" she murmured.

"I've been trained to be a good observer," he said. "Just ease in slowly—there's no hurry. We'll keep the windows open. Okay, here we go."

He offered her his hand and helped her into the car. For a moment, Erica's head swam with dizziness as she settled herself on the soft, supple leather. Then she gulped a few breaths of air and felt better. Her smile up at Gray was tentative.

"So far, so good," she said.

"All right, I'm going to close the door now." First he rolled down the window. "Easy does it."

He shut the door, then walked around to the driver's side and got in. Rolling down his own window, he looked over at her.

In the small space, their heads were close together. Erica noticed for the first time that tiny chips of gold gleamed in the depths of Gray's cognac-colored eyes. The golden chips reminded her of carefree summer days spent playing beside sun-dappled streams, where shiny pebbles glittered like coins. Such childhood memories always gave Erica a dreamy sensation, as if she were floating through time on a lovely, soft cloud.

"Are you all right?" said Gray.

He was staring back at her, an expression of mild concern on his face. Erica quickly looked away and forced herself to gaze through the windshield.

"I'm fine," she fibbed, for her heart was doing back-flips.

How embarrassing to have been caught staring at Gray like a schoolgirl. Good grief, what must he think?

"I—I feel a little breathless," she went on, "but I'll be okay."

In truth, Erica was beginning to wonder if she'd ever be okay again, after having met Gray. For the second time, she wondered if she was attracted to the man simply because he was her doctor. Of course, he wasn't officially her doctor anymore, but that was beside the point. Her feelings confused her, especially in light of the fact that she and

Gray were on opposite sides of a controversy that could very easily evolve into an ugly battle royal.

"I guess cars aren't going to be a problem for me," she continued, focusing on a less discomfiting subject. "Just keep these windows open." She laughed self-consciously.

Gray turned the ignition key. The Jaguar's engine hummed into life with the soft purr of a fine machine that's kept in perfect running order. They backed out of the parking slot, and Erica gave Gray directions to her houseboat on Lake Union.

As they drove, Erica noticed that she felt no hint of panic. Resting her arm on the sill of the open window, she mulled the situation over and tried to remain positive. Perhaps what had happened back at the hospital would never occur again. Even so, she vowed to stay out of elevators for the next few days.

"It's almost noon," said Gray, glancing at his watch. "No wonder I'm hungry. May I buy you lunch?"

Erica grasped at this opportunity. Gray had done so much for her, the least she could do was treat him to lunch.

"Food sounds great," she said, "and I'll buy." She waved off his protests. "No, I insist." An idea had formed in her mind. "Turn left at the next corner," she said. "I know of a wonderful little take-out deli that makes the best sandwiches in Seattle. I'll run in and get us a couple, plus some other goodies—you won't believe their cheesecake—then we can eat on the deck at my place."

"Good plan," said Gray, flashing her a smile.

Suddenly Erica felt better—happier and more at peace—than she'd felt since her accident. Quickly she analyzed her emotions. The wonderful weather was certainly a contributing factor. It was a gorgeous summer day in her beautiful adopted city. The sunshine gleamed on Lake Union, and a slight breeze was causing the colored pennants on the sailboats to flutter like flower petals.

As a warm current of air caressed her skin, Erica pondered the fact that she'd been given a priceless second chance at life. That was no small matter. She felt sure that every time she thought about Gray's selfless act from then on, her spirits would get a lift.

Beautiful weather. A second chance at life. But there was something else, Erica was certain. What was it?

She stole a secret glance at Gray. His strong masculine profile was silhouetted against the blue lake, whose rippled surface suggested crushed velvet. The smooth, relaxed expression on Gray's wide brow and the smiling corners of his eyes revealed that he felt as easy in Erica's company at that moment as she felt in his.

Erica continued her assessment, feeling drawn in by the vision. She noted how Gray's firm wrists flexed when he negotiated a turn. His strong, tanned fingers curved around the leather-covered steering wheel in a way that suggested both power and sensitivity—a heady mixture. As she'd done before, Erica pictured those capable hands in a myriad of tasks and wondered how it would feel to have them stroke her hair or skin.

She dragged her eyes away and drew in some steadying breaths between parted lips. Why did her thoughts keep straying into such suggestive territory? she wondered. Hopefully, Gray wasn't a mind-reader, or he'd get quite a surprise.

Then it occurred to her that he might at that very moment

be thinking about tearing down the Wagner House and putting up a hideous modern building in its place. The mental image of a glass-and-concrete monstrosity rising where the graceful old house had once stood made Erica frown with distaste.

Just then, Gray's voice broke in on Erica's disquieting thoughts.

"Is this the place?" he asked, pulling up in front of a shop named Frank's Deli.

"Yes, this is it," said Erica thankfully, the spell of her reverie of mixed emotions broken. She grabbed her purse and escaped from the car, away from Gray's disturbing presence.

Soon they were seated at a table on the back deck of Erica's houseboat. Laughing and talking at once, they spread their feast out before them. As they opened the containers of potato salad and cole slaw and unwrapped the sandwiches and pickles, Gray seemed as eager as a hungry bear who's just found a honey tree. His unself-conscious enthusiasm for one of life's simple pleasures delighted Erica.

They ate in silence for a few minutes, then Gray spoke.

"I like it here," he said, looking around. "It must be fun living on a houseboat."

"Oh, it is," said Erica, helping herself to another pickle. "As soon as I saw this place, I fell in love with it. I'm sure I wouldn't have been this happy in an apartment."

"What's the best part?" asked Gray. "The great surroundings?" He indicated the beautiful blue lake overhung with a canopy-sky dotted with puffy clouds.

"Yes, there's that, of course," said Erica in a thoughtful

tone. "But mostly it's about the sensation of freedom that I get whenever I'm here. It's actually quite similar to how I feel when I'm flying."

"How so?" said Gray, regarding her with curiosity.

"Well," said Erica, "when you live on a houseboat, the scene outside is always changing. I never know what I'll see when I look out the window: Boats, geese, swimmers. It's different all the time—I love the endless variety." She paused. "It's the same when I'm flying. I get that wonderful feeling of freedom and adventure. Every time I go up, there's something new and fascinating to look at or learn about." She smiled. "Sometimes when I'm falling asleep and the house is gently rocking, it feels just like being in a small plane—it's great."

"Hmm, that's very interesting," said Gray, nodding. "I never would have thought of it in those terms."

"Actually, neither had I," said Erica, giving a little shrug. "It was a happy discovery." She passed him the container of cole slaw. "Want some more?"

"Thanks, I'm fine," said Gray. He wiped his lips with the cloth napkin that Erica had provided, then added, "You were certainly right about the food—that was wonderful. How could I live in Seattle and not know about Frank's Deli?"

"In your profession, you probably don't get many chances to discover new places," said Erica. "You must be terribly busy."

"Yes," said Gray, with a rueful nod, "my schedule does tend to be a little crowded. I lead a hectic life, but I think that's about to change, thank goodness."

Erica regarded him curiously. Before she had a chance to ask him to elaborate, however, he spoke again.

"Hey, look, we've got company," said Gray, nodding toward the water beyond the deck railing.

Some mallard ducks were swimming up to the houseboat. Beads of moisture glistened on their backs as they bobbed on the gentle swells. The ducks eyed the diners and quacked softly.

"See what I mean?" said Erica, laughing. "Different all the time."

"How can you resist these moochers?" said Gray.

"I can't," said Erica, standing up. "I adore having ducks swim right up to my house. I'll get them something to eat."

Soon she returned with some stale dinner rolls. Gray reached for one and joined Erica at the railing, where they tossed bits of bread to the ducks until the rolls were gone.

Resuming their seats, Gray and Erica sat back and relaxed for the better part of an hour, chatting about nothing in particular as they gazed at Lake Union and the surrounding Seattle skyline. A man and woman paddled by in a canoe and exchanged waves with them. Some small sailboats skimmed the surface out in the middle of the lake, and a little flock of Canada geese circled overhead before alighting on the water amid splashes and a chorus of honking.

Presently, a Siamese cat belonging to one of Erica's neighbors jumped aboard and approached Gray and Erica, meowing for attention. Her name was Sophie and she was a frequent visitor to Erica's houseboat. Gray leaned over and scooped her up.

"Well, hello there," he said. He settled the animal on his lap and began scratching behind her ears.

Watching Gray pet Sophie, Erica felt an intense throb of attraction toward him. His fingers moved so sensuously in the silken fur on the cat's head and neck, she found herself wishing that she, instead of the obviously enchanted Sophie, were at the receiving end of Gray's attentiveness.

Just then Gray raised his head and looked over at Erica. His fingers stopped moving for a moment as a gleam of interest lit up his eyes. He'd caught Erica staring at him again, and this time he seemed to have guessed what sort of thoughts were cavorting in her mind. The mellow air between them suddenly sizzled with a pleasant kind of tension.

A tremor swept through Erica's body. Attempting to cover up her flustered state, she fell back on her role as hostess.

"Are you ready for dessert and coffee?" she asked. Maddeningly, her voice shook.

"I'm in no hurry," he said, slanting her a smile that spread slowly over his face like warm honey. "Let's wait." He set Sophie onto the deck.

Although their conversation that afternoon had been light and casual, and had mercifully stayed off the hot topic of the Wagner House—so far—there was nothing casual about the way Gray's eyes were just then gazing at Erica. Normally, such frank male appraisal made Erica feel as if she were being coolly sized up as a commodity on the dating-and-mating market. Gray's lingering, inoffensive glance, however, suggested nothing of the kind. That he admired her was obvious—his appreciative expression said it all.

"You know, I could go for a glass of ice water, though,"

he said. "It's getting pretty warm out here." So saying, he slipped off his sports jacket and rolled up his shirt sleeves.

"Ice water coming right up," said Erica, standing. This was just the little break she needed in order to regain her inner composure. "I think I'll get into something more comfortable while I'm at it," she added and headed inside.

A few minutes later, Erica had changed into some shorts and a strapless bandeau made of soft, stretchy fabric. Over these she wore an oversized shirt, which she'd left loose and unbuttoned. In the kitchen, she filled two tumblers with ice, added water and some lemon slices, then walked back outside.

Gray was standing at the far end of the deck, having an animated conversation with a man in a kayak. Rather than interrupt, Erica busied herself with a couple of thick lounging cushions, which she pulled from a storage bin. The sun-heated wood of the deck felt wonderfully warm on the soles of her bare feet. Looking around with pleasure, she reflected at how lucky she had been to get such a prime location. Her houseboat was at the end of the float, which gave her an unobstructed view plus added privacy.

The deck was alive with vibrant color, for Erica, who loved flowers, had brought gardening to her floating home. Several terra-cotta pots and wooden half-barrels overflowed with petunias and geraniums. A trembling profusion of sweet peas festooned a trellis, their perfume scenting the summer air. Some golden honeybees buzzed among the blossoms.

Erica arranged the cushions side by side on the deck and sat down on one of them. The sun's warm rays felt heavenly on the top of her head and along her shoulders and arms. She shook out her hair and let the breeze lift it off her neck. The houseboat rocked gently. Bending her legs, she clasped her hands around her knees, savoring the moment. Life was sweet.

Just then, a tall shadow slanted across the deck as Gray turned from the railing and walked over to join her. The man in the kayak was paddling away.

Erica looked up and smiled, her eyes taking in Gray's broad shoulders and well-proportioned forearms. Even though he was clad in a shirt and slacks, Erica was aware that his physique was not that of an overdeveloped weight lifter, but was toned and solid, every ounce of muscle and sinew at the peak of fitness.

Gray's strides toward her rolled easily from his lean hips. His was a confident, economical gait that suggested leashed power laced with a potent dash of masculinity. Erica was once again reminded of a lone and lawless cowboy who made up his own rules—and let the devil take the hindmost.

She shivered, even as a flush warmed the skin of her neck. She was sure that Gray was unaware that the way his body moved when he walked could conjure up such images, just as he seemed oblivious to every other superficial detail about himself. He wore his clothes—and his skin— in a completely unself-conscious way, a fact that made him all the more attractive, reflected Erica.

"It's a small world," said Gray, chuckling.

"What do you mean?" said Erica.

"That guy has a kayak just like mine," said Gray. "It's an unusual model, so we were comparing notes." Then he quirked a smile at her. "Sorry to keep you waiting."

"Not at all," said Erica. "Have some water."

"Thanks," he said and took a long drink from the glass she'd handed to him. "Ah, that's just what I needed."

He sat beside her on the other cushion, then reached over and tugged at the sleeve of her voluminous shirt.

"Why are you so bundled up?" he said with a teasing smile. "After a week in the hospital, I should think you'd want to catch a few rays."

"I still have some bruises from the accident," said Erica, dipping her head. She hated the thought of Gray seeing the discolorations on her skin.

"There's no need to be embarrassed about that," said Gray kindly. "Come on," he said, "take this thing off." He eased her shirt from her shoulders and down her arms. "Relax and get some sun. It'll do you good."

He put the shirt to one side and scanned her body. Was it merely professional interest? wondered Erica. There was a bruise on her upper arm. It had faded from an angry purple to a paler hue. Gray lightly touched the spot.

"Does it still hurt?" he asked.

"Mmm, a little," said Erica.

"Well, that's normal," said Gray. "You're definitely on the mend, though. In a day or so, these will be just a memory."

Gray continued to study her. His eyes took in the clingy bandeau, which molded to her form like a second skin. Visually he traced the vulnerable curves of her uncovered shoulders, her slender neck, her bare thighs and calves. Then he reached over and, with a light but lingering touch, brushed the back of his fingers along her cheek.

"Lovely lady," he said, his voice a caress, "bruises or not, you're disturbingly attractive."

Erica hardly knew what to say. Anything she might have murmured in response stuck in her throat. Her lips parted and a little sigh escaped.

"I have a confession to make," continued Gray.

His brown eyes seemed to penetrate into Erica's soul, burning straight through her like a gaze distilled from fine whiskey.

"What do you mean?" asked Erica.

"You were a tough case for me, back there in the hospital," said Gray. "You looked so fragile when we brought you in." His eyes lightly roved over her face, pausing at her brow, her lips, her hair that was softly stirring against her skin. A palpable aura of mutual attraction throbbed in the air. Gray went on.

"I found myself caring too much about what happened to you," he said. "It's one thing to be concerned about a patient—that's our job—but it's best to keep a certain emotional distance." He smiled ruefully. "We doctors wouldn't survive if we didn't." He paused. "But in your case, it was very hard to watch you lying in that bed unconscious and as pale and still as death." His voice had grown husky. "You were so helpless, so vulnerable that first twenty-four hours." He gently brushed some hair from her brow. "I'm not used to getting drawn in like that." He chuckled briefly. "It was a little disconcerting."

Then, as if realizing that he'd revealed too much about himself, Gray turned away, cleared his throat, and abruptly changed the subject.

"Let's talk about the Wagner House for a minute," he said, squinting out at the water.

"I was afraid you'd eventually bring that up," said Erica with a little groan.

"That horrible old eyesore—"

"Hey," interrupted Erica, "watch your language."

"But it *is* an eyesore," said Gray. "Anyone can see that."

"What I see," said Erica, "is an elegant old house from a bygone era. All it needs is a little work to bring it back to its former glory."

"Well, you have the bygone-era part right, anyway," said Gray, with an ironic twist of his mouth. "That's a prime piece of property, Erica, and it's handily located right near the hospital. It needs to be cleared to make room for a building that is part of *this* era, one that will serve today's community. What we don't need taking up that space is a down-at-the-heels relic from the past."

"I am just amazed at you," said Erica, moving an inch or two away from Gray in order to turn and look at him.

"What do you mean?"

"I thought you were appalled by Seattle's growth spurt."

"I am," said Gray, looking puzzled. "But what does that have to do with this?"

"The Wagner House is part of the past," said Erica, "part of that small-town feeling you told me you so terribly miss."

"Oh, no," said Gray, shaking his head, "this is different."

"How so?"

"It's progress," he said. "This is not about too many people in Puget Sound. It's about using land to its best advantage."

"What *is* your project, by the way?" said Erica, curiosity overriding her annoyance for a moment.

"I'm putting up a building that will house some individual doctors' offices," said Gray, "as well as a new crisis clinic."

"A crisis clinic?" said Erica, her interest piqued.

"That's right," said Gray. "The old crisis clinic has outgrown its present location, and Seattle will be better served if we can provide a new facility."

"Hmm."

"Have I convinced you?" asked Gray, regarding her.

"No," said Erica firmly, "you've just given me food for thought, that's all."

"Care to elaborate?"

"Not at the moment," said Erica, "and, anyway, what difference would it make? We're not going to agree about this, and you can be sure that the Board is going to hold its ground. We'll fight you in the courts, if necessary." She paused, letting her words sink in. "You'll just have to put your new building somewhere else."

"We'll see about that," said Gray, his eyes reflecting flames of determination and suppressed combat. Clearly, he had just begun his campaign to bring Erica over to his side. For the moment, however, he seemed willing to put the subject on the back burner. His and Erica's difference of opinions, after all, was putting a blight on the beautiful afternoon.

A few moments of uneasy silence ticked by, the tension eventually draining away as they watched a little Foss tugboat that was chugging past. The tug's cook was standing in the stern, tossing scraps to some swooping gulls. Ripples from the craft splashed against the float, causing the house-boat to rock gently on the swells.

Farther out in the lake, a man dove from a pleasure craft. Rising to the surface, he strongly stroked the water and began swimming laps. Shading her eyes as she watched him, Erica was reminded of the day that Gray had plunged into Lake Washington and pulled her from the sinking helicopter. Once again, her heart spilled over with gratitude. She broke the silence.

"That man swimming out there makes me think of how you saved my life," she said.

"Now don't go all gushy on me," said Gray, wagging a finger at her in mock rebuke.

As before, Erica reflected that Gray seemed ill at ease with the subject of his brave deed. Wanting to reassure him, she decided to use humor to defuse any discomfort he might feel about the topic.

"You can't blame me for feeling some hero worship for you," she said lightly. "Think of what you did for me. Why, it's only natural that I—"

And then she could've bitten her tongue, for Gray's re-action was swift and decisive.

"Don't call me a hero," he interrupted, holding up a hand to halt her flow of words.

Erica studied him and was startled to see a sudden in-tensity of emotion burning in the depths of his eyes, like fires smoldering on a scarred battlefield. She could almost smell the smoke.

"Please don't ever call me that again," he repeated.

He spoke softly from between tight lips, reminding Erica of a blade concealed beneath velvet. A nerve twitched in his jaw and his eyes bored into her from beneath lowered brows. Clearly, Erica had unwittingly tapped into a reservoir of pain that Gray held deep within himself.

"Gray," she said kindly, "what is it?"

"Don't apply hero worship to me," he said. "Someone else once pinned that label on me and it cost her dearly." His eyes flickered with remembered sorrow and his voice was harsh with regret. "I swore then that I'd never let anyone put me in that position again."

"I'm sorry," said Erica softly. "I—I didn't know."

Chapter Six

"I'm sorry, Gray," Erica repeated. "I certainly didn't mean to bring up bad memories for you."

Her curiosity was naturally piqued by Gray's reference to another woman, but Erica's intuition told her that this was not the time to pry, however gently, into his personal life. She wondered, though, if he was referring to one of his patients. Or, was he perhaps talking about the woman he'd once been engaged to, the one that Leslie, the nurse, had mentioned?

"Oh, it's okay," said Gray, breaking in on her thoughts. "It isn't your fault." His tone lightened. "But don't make me into a hero or some kind of superman. Believe me, I'm neither one of those. Here, I'll prove it to you."

He opened his shirt and showed her a faint scar on his chest. Several inches in length, it angled across his skin, right above his heart.

"Oh, my goodness," murmured Erica.

She spontaneously reached out to lightly touch the spot, and felt Gray's strong pulse beating beneath her fingers. Catching her breath, she withdrew her hand.

"I'm only human," he said, rebuttoning his shirt. "When I'm cut, I bleed."

"How did you get that scar?" she said.

"I had an accident a few years ago," he said, "while floating the Yukon River. I almost died." He dipped his head toward her. "So you see, I'm mortal, just like you and everyone else."

At that moment, any remaining awkwardness between them vanished as Gray's eyes drifted downward, pausing to watch the pulse fluttering like a captured moth in the hollow of Erica's throat. Like a connoisseur of fine things, he gazed long and lingeringly, as if the living landscape of Erica's form pleased him and drew him on. Then, bending closer, he kissed her.

For one surprised moment, Erica felt as if the air had been snatched from her lungs. Gray's mouth slanted over hers, his lips taking full possession with a confidence that inflamed her senses. She'd been wondering how Gray's mustache would feel on her skin—now she knew. The soft, curving hairs brushed against her with a pleasing tickle. At that moment, it seemed the most natural thing in the world to reach up and encircle Gray's neck with her arms.

Encouraged by Erica's response, Gray murmured deep in his throat as his kiss intensified. With a sense of heightened awareness, Erica reveled in the touch of Gray's lips caressing hers with a silken mastery that left her gasping.

When at last their lips parted, Gray gazed into Erica's

eyes, seeming to note that her skin was flushed with excitement. His fingers sifted through her hair, then he lifted the heavy blond tresses to his face and breathed deeply, as if savoring an intoxicating fragrance.

"Oh, Erica," he murmured, and kissed her again.

Erica surrendered herself to the moment, swept up in a tidal wave of pleasurable feelings, as Gray seared a line of kisses down her neck and along her collarbone. His arms clasped her in a protective embrace, his exploring lips caressed her sun-warmed skin, and his hair brushed against her in a silken sweep.

"How sweet you are," he whispered near her ear.

As Erica responded to Gray's kisses like a rose opening to an insistent, nuzzling bee, she felt the passionate side of her personality rise to the surface. Gray's aura of masculinity was a stunning presence, one that was awakening her as surely as if she'd been Sleeping Beauty. She sighed deeply as his lips scorched a path across her sensitive skin. Here indeed was a man who savored life and embraced its many aspects with unabashed gusto. With deep feminine instinct, Erica knew that Gray was not afraid to unleash the powerful emotions that have drawn men and women together since the beginning of time.

Presently, however, a warning bell went off in Erica's brain. Although her deck was relatively private from the neighboring houseboats, it was nevertheless visible from the water and to any boaters that happened to pass by. In any case, it was time to call things to a halt.

"Gray," she said.

"Mmm?" he said, burying his face in her hair.

"We'd better stop," she said, still breathless, "or I'll think you're trying to completely sweep me off my feet."

"Sounds like a good idea," he said, playfully growling against her neck.

"Besides," she added, "you and I probably shouldn't become romantically involved. All things considered."

"We're not going to let an old house come between us," he said with quiet emphasis, "if that's what you mean."

"But we're on different sides of the issue and—"

"Shh," he said and lightly kissed her on the tip of her nose. "We can discuss that another time." Just then, he glanced at his watch. "Oh, good grief," he said, standing up.

"What is it?" said Erica, getting to her feet, as well.

"I forgot I have a meeting today," said Gray. "I'd better call and tell them I'm running late. May I use your phone?"

"Yes, of course," said Erica. "It's on the bookcase."

A few minutes later, Gray returned to the deck and reached for his jacket. His face wore a back-to-business expression.

"Thanks for the lunch," he said, with a distracted smile. "I'm sorry to have to dash off like this." Then he looked at her, his eyes still glowing from their intimate embraces. "I want to see you again, Erica," he said earnestly.

"I don't know," she said, hesitating, for she was torn between her attraction to him and her outrage over his plan for the Wagner House.

"Erica," he said simply, taking her hand and pressing her fingers to his lips. His eyes implored her.

"Oh, all right," she said, laughing. "Who could resist such a look?"

"It's just my boyish charm," he teased. Then he took out

his car keys, adding, "I'll give you a call." He started to leave, then turned to regard her once more.

"Look," he said, "there's something I want you to do before I go."

"What is it?"

"I want you to make me a promise," said Gray. He raised one eyebrow. "You probably won't like it, but it's for your own good."

"I don't understand," said Erica, feeling wary. "What kind of promise?" What was Gray leading up to?

"I don't want you to do any flying for a while," he said.

"Oh, not that subject again," she replied, taking offense. She crossed her arms over her chest and slid her eyes toward the glittering water. "I was hoping you'd dropped it."

"I know you're determined to get back up there," he said, jerking a thumb skyward. "I can't stop you—it's your life. But that little episode in the elevator should've told you something."

"Yes, it did," said Erica, feeling a renewed call to conflict churning in her stomach. "It told me that I've got a challenge ahead of me, maybe more of one than I thought at first. But I don't mind," she added with a show of spirit.

"At least promise me that you'll stay grounded for the next few days," said Gray.

"I won't be doing the traffic report for a while," she said, "but that doesn't mean I won't be flying at all."

"I'm afraid for your safety," responded Gray. "What if you have another panic attack while you're in the air? Besides, you need time to catch your breath and sort out your feelings," he insisted.

When Erica remained silent, he plowed his fingers through his hair in a burst of exasperation.

"Why won't you listen to me, you stubborn woman?" he said, half seriously, half in jest.

"I don't back away from challenges," retorted Erica, who was unmoved by Gray's impassioned words. "And I'm not on anyone's leash, certainly not yours. Just because you saved my life doesn't mean you own it."

"Of course it doesn't," Gray flung back at her.

"When you had your accident on the Yukon River," said Erica, "did you stop traveling to remote corners of the world because of it?"

"Well, no, but—"

"It's the same for me," said Erica, "don't you see? I can't let one accident and a freak fainting spell hold me back. I refuse to be defeated by fear."

"I admire your spunk," said Gray, "but you're being unrealistic." He stepped closer and gazed into her eyes. "Look, if you won't do it for yourself, do it as a personal favor for me. Promise me that you won't fly for one week. Give me that, Erica."

Erica parted her lips to refuse him, and then she caught the genuine look of concern in his eyes. She waged a short inner battle with her pride and finally decided to give in to Gray. After all, what was one week?

"Oh, all right," she said, throwing up her hands in defeat. "I promise not to fly for one week."

Gray nodded his satisfaction. Then, glancing at his watch, he said, "I really have to go." He took a few steps away from her, adding, "I figured that your initial reaction would be negative, but I also think that you're basically a reasonable person. I know you'll see things my way, once you've thought about it."

"Thanks for the vote of confidence," she said, her voice laced with sarcasm.

"Okay," said Gray, holding up his hand in a gesture of surrender, "so I'm not the world's most diplomatic person." He regarded her. "I'm glad I finally got you to agree, that's all."

"Just remember," said Erica, aiming an accusing look at him, "you dragged it out of me."

"Yeah, okay," muttered Gray, his tone of voice indicating that their exchange had been no picnic for him, either. Then he sketched a hasty wave in the air and turned to leave. "I'll be in touch," he tossed over his shoulder.

Don't bother, Erica almost shouted after him with residual anger, but she somehow managed to keep her tongue in check.

She watched him walk along the float with rapid strides until he disappeared from view. Then she let out a sigh of frustration and began clearing the table. The afternoon had taken a couple of unpleasant turns and she regretted that. For instance, how could Gray kiss and embrace her one minute, then impose his I-know-what's-best-for-you-even-if-you-don't attitude on her the next? It was annoying, to say the least.

Then there was the fact that Gray was intent on tearing down the very Seattle landmark that Erica had vowed to save. For a few minutes that afternoon, while nestled in Gray's arms, Erica had entertained the possibility of a blossoming romance between her and Gray—one step at a time, of course. But now, she couldn't imagine how the two of them could be on opposing sides of such a hot issue as the Wagner House controversy, at the heart of which were different values, and at the same time pursue a loving relationship. In Erica's mind, such elements seemed to cancel each other out.

She stacked the dishes, her irritation expressing itself in the sharp clink of the plates as they knocked together. Next, the flatware clattered onto the china, causing Sophie, who'd been napping in the sun, to awaken with a start and stalk away with an air of feline disgruntlement.

"Sorry, Sophie," said Erica to the departing cat.

Erica jammed the empty salad containers together, then paused for a moment. Presently calmer, she stared out at the water and gave in to her musings. There were things about Gray that definitely stirred her interest, she had to admit. Her lips still tingled from his kisses, but Erica wanted to know more about him than how he kissed and how he felt in her arms. Questions about him glanced off the inner corridors of her mind. For one thing, he'd hinted that his hectic lifestyle was about to change. What had he meant by that? she wondered. His comment about a woman from his past made her especially curious. How had someone's hero worship for Gray cost that person dearly, as he'd put it?

Erica picked up the dishes and headed for the kitchen. Maybe she'd never know the answers to any of her questions. Probably the best thing was not to see Gray again, even though she'd already agreed to do so. She'd have to think about that.

Early that evening, a delivery man arrived with the empty Chinese vase in which Gray had given Erica the blue irises. Erica paid the man, closed the door, and then stood in the hallway, simply staring at the vase in her hands. Her emotions were still unsettled and, feeling a burst of pique, she very nearly thrust the vase into a dark closet where she wouldn't have to look at it.

Then, without warning, her eyes filled with tears of gratitude, for the vase was a powerful physical reminder of what Gray had done for her. Slowly she walked into the living room. She set the vase in a place of honor on top of an oak buffet, then stood back to admire its elegant shape and its blue-and-white design. Whatever else she might think of Gray, the fact remained that he'd saved her life. She'd never be able to forget that.

Sometime during the still, dark hours before dawn the next morning, Erica began tossing in her sleep. Disturbing images cavorted in her mind, like sinister imps bent on snatching away her peace. She dreamed that she was running in slow motion through a dense, primeval forest. The broad limbs of huge conifers were intertwined overhead, casting inky shadows onto the cone-littered ground. Erica's feet and legs felt as if they were encased in concrete as she struggled to outrun the unnamed terror—a presence as hot and malevolent as dragon breath—that was pressing at her back.

In her dream, Erica cried out and closed her eyes to blot out her surroundings. Suddenly, she was falling . . . falling . . . and the earth spun. She knew that as long as she kept her eyes closed, she'd be all right, but if she opened them, she'd plunge into water and drown. Something soft yet unyielding, like a padded wall, began crowding in on her from all sides. She couldn't breathe. She was falling and suffocating at the same time. There was no way out. She was about to die.

Erica's cries of terror awoke her. Panic-stricken, she sat bolt upright in her bed, bathed in perspiration. Trying to banish the frightening images from her spinning mind, she switched on her bedside lamp with trembling fingers. She looked around to reassure herself that she was safe in her bedroom, amidst familiar surroundings. Water gently lapped against the houseboat, and she could hear the plaintive fluting of a night bird passing overhead.

Shivering, Erica pulled the covers around her. The images in her dream had been very disturbing, but worst of all had been the trapped, panicky sensation that had occurred at the end. Falling with her eyes closed, she'd felt exactly as she had when the helicopter was tumbling toward the lake.

She sipped from a glass of water beside her bed and turned off the light. Lying back down and tucking the covers under her chin, she tried to calm herself. After all, it had only been a bad dream—she mustn't read too much into it. Everyone had nightmares now and then. Besides, dreams about falling were to be expected after her harrowing experience in the chopper.

Still, she couldn't help but wonder when she'd shake off the effects of the crash. How would she be able to get on with her life if she was forced to relive that same terrifying scene over and over again?

On her way home from running errands later that morning, Erica bought some flowers for the vase that Gray had given to her. Back at her houseboat, as she was arranging the fragrant blooms, an idea began tugging at the corners of her mind. When Marty, her boss, had insisted that she take a few extra days off, it had seemed like a good plan at the time. Erica hadn't anticipated, though, how quickly she'd become restless and want to return to work. In fact, she was itching to get back into her normal routine.

Putting the finishing touches on the bouquet, she realized that part of her restlessness was due to a burning curiosity: How would she react when she climbed back into the small confines of a helicopter for the first time? Would she panic? Would she feel faint and dizzy? Would her palms sweat and her stomach churn with remembered terror?

There was only one way to find out.

Her mind made up, Erica wiped her hands and reached for her purse and jacket. Firmly closing the front door behind her, she strode up the float toward her car, her steps full of purpose. She'd go to KMBR's rooftop heliport, borrow one of the choppers, and take the most important flight of her life.

Her stomach fluttered with nervous excitement as she thought about her experiment. So much seemed to ride on the outcome. If all went well and she had no panic attacks, she'd ask Marty to put her back into the air immediately.

But what if things didn't go well?

Banishing such thoughts from her mind, Erica took a deep breath, slid behind the wheel of her car, and thrust her key into the ignition.

Just then she paused, recalling the promise that Gray had wrung out of her the day before. What would his reaction be once he learned that she'd flown so soon after the accident, in spite of his dire warnings not to?

Erica lifted her chin, engaged the engine, and shifted the car into gear. So she'd changed her mind, she thought with a spurt of rebelliousness. After all, she'd given the promise under protest. Besides, it had supposedly been for her good, not Gray's. Only she knew what was best for her. And what was best for her now—this minute—was to look her fear squarely in the eye. Last night's bad dream had underscored that urgent need.

"She who hesitates is lost," she murmured with a will and pulled away from the curb.

And if Gray later called her action impulsive and reckless, well, that was his problem.

Chapter Seven

A couple of hours later, the weather had changed dramatically. In typical Northwest fashion, the sunshine that had greeted Erica that morning had been swallowed up, and the temperature had dropped into the cool zone. In the sun's place was a somber mantle of leaden clouds that smudged the sky and cast a pall on the earth. Lake Union mirrored the sullen ash color of the sky, and its surface heaved in restless anticipation of the coming storm.

Thunder rumbled in the distance and some fat raindrops spattered onto the float as Erica hastened toward her houseboat. The dry stalks of a neighbor's potted bamboo rattled against each other in the fretting breeze as she passed by. Keeping her head down, Erica unlocked her door and ducked inside. She shut the door behind her, then shrugged out of her jacket and tossed it onto a chair in an uncharacteristic gesture of carelessness. She stood in the middle of the room for a few moments, not moving. Then with heavy steps she walked to an overstuffed chair, sank down onto it, and stared out at the agitated water.

Erica's mood matched the gloomy weather. With dejected eyes, she watched a sparkling limb of lightning appear and then fade on the horizon. Thunder rumbled again, closer this time. The world seemed to hold its breath and darken. Then there came a staccato drumbeat on the roof, and the somber lake began to dimple with raindrops.

Erica's vision of the storm-battered window blurred as tears spilled out of her eyes and coursed down her cheeks. She didn't even bother to wipe them away as she sat in a state of numb disappointment, her hands motionless on the arms of her chair. For several minutes she remained in this attitude of abject discouragement, letting her inner storm burst forth and expend itself. Crying wouldn't change what had happened, but it might help ease some of her pain.

As the storm outside let up a little, Erica's sobbing subsided as well and finally stopped. Getting to her feet, she went into the bathroom, re-emerging with a handful of tissues. Sinking back onto her chair, she wiped her tear-stained face and blew her nose. She hadn't felt that low in a long time. As if mesmerized, she watched the rain as it splashed onto the deck and dripped from the railing.

Just then the telephone rang. Erica jumped at the sound, her nerves on edge. She looked at the phone, debating whether to respond to its intrusive summons or let her machine record a message. In her present state of mind, there was really no one she wanted to talk to. On the other hand, hearing someone else's voice might be just the distraction she needed.

She reached for the phone, sniffling one last time as she tried to compose herself. Taking a deep breath, she picked up the receiver.

"Hello?"

"Hello, Erica," responded a familiar masculine voice. "It's Gray. I'm just calling to see how you're doing."

For a moment, everything flew out of Erica's mind except for the realization of how good it felt to hear from Gray. The rich, deep tones traveling along the phone line seemed to caress her ear.

"I'm doing great," she fibbed and forced herself to smile as she said it.

"I'm glad to hear that," said Gray, then added, "Oh, hang on a second, will you?" Then he said off to one side, "Yes, nurse, that'll be fine. Hand me a pen and I'll sign this." Pause. "Okay, there you go." His voice came back on the line. "Sorry," he said. "I should know better than to make phone calls near a nurses' station. My shift's over and I'm headed for the gym. I was wondering if you'd have dinner with me tonight."

"I guess I could," said Erica a bit hesitantly.

"Is that a yes or a no?" asked Gray, with a chuckle.

"Oh, yes, I suppose," said Erica.

"Look, I realize our last encounter ended on a somewhat ragged note," said Gray in a cajoling tone, "but couldn't you muster a little more enthusiasm?"

There was a pause.

"Erica?"

"I'm here," she said. "I just wonder if we should be seeing each other, that's all. We do have a certain conflict of interests, in case you've forgotten."

"I haven't forgotten," said Gray, "but I'll tell you what: Tonight at dinner I'll let you make your case for saving the Wagner House. I promise to listen patiently and consider the Board's point of view. That's my best offer," he added with a short laugh, "so what do you say?"

"I accept your invitation," she said, her mind already on how best to present Gray with the facts as she saw them. She knew that he was not an entirely unreasonable man; perhaps tonight she could persuade him to rethink his plan and not destroy the Wagner House, after all.

"Good, that's settled," he said. "I'll pick you up around seven. Oh, by the way, have you had any more panic episodes?"

Erica hesitated, dismayed to feel her throat tightening. She really didn't want to lose her composure and break down again with Gray on the phone. Feminine tears and heavy emotional scenes had always baffled and unnerved the men she had dated in the past, and she assumed that Gray would be just as put off if she started crying. Besides, she knew what he'd say if he found out she'd flown that afternoon.

Quickly she cast about for a light comment that would lead the conversation away from the topic of panic attacks. But she'd hesitated a heartbeat too long.

"Erica?"

She could hear the edge in Gray's voice. He knew that something was wrong. And, like an alert bloodhound, he would be difficult to put off the trail.

"What's going on?" he demanded. "Why aren't you answering me?"

Erica tried to swallow the sob that was welling up in her

constricted throat, but she was only partially successful. To her chagrin, her eyes once more filled with tears.

"Oh, I may as well tell you now and get it over with," she said with an air of resignation. "You'd probably find out about it anyway."

"Find out about what?" said Gray.

Erica felt a nervous, queasy fluttering in the pit of her stomach. Gray reminded her just then of a coach who suspects that a member of his team has broken a serious training rule. Mustering her courage, she plunged ahead anyway.

"I flew today," she blurted.

Then she could've bitten her tongue as she listened to Gray's heavy, incredulous silence smoke along the telephone line.

"You did what?" he finally said, raising his voice.

"I flew one of the station's choppers today," she repeated, twisting the phone cord. "Be happy for me, Gray. At least I faced my fear. Now I know exactly what I'm up against. Yes, I had a panic attack, but the chopper landed safely and I'm fine." She paused to dry her eyes. "Or, I will be."

"You didn't fly by yourself, I hope," said Gray.

"No," said Erica, "I took another pilot up with me, just in case."

"Well, thank goodness for that, at least," said Gray, "but it was still an idiotic thing to do, in my opinion. Tell me what happened."

"I was at the controls," said Erica, "and I clutched up—fear, dizziness, sick to my stomach—just like in the elevator." She took a deep breath. "Anyway, the other pilot took over and flew the chopper back to the station. I couldn't wait to get out of that thing."

"You promised me that you weren't going to fly for a while," said Gray.

"I'm sorry," said Erica. "I don't usually break my word, but I regret having made that promise. I gave it under duress, if you'll recall."

"Yes, I remember having to twist your arm," said Gray, most of the irritation gone from his voice. He sighed and went on. "Well, I suppose I can understand your wanting to test your reactions up in the air. I'm sorry things didn't work out for you."

"Thanks," said Erica, touched by his expression of sympathy and support.

"I suppose you're thinking you'll never fly again," said Gray.

"It's crossed my mind," she said, in rueful understatement.

"Be patient, Erica. Just take it one day at a time."

"I guess I'll have to," she said in a small voice.

Just then, a completely different topic entered her mind. She latched on to it, grateful to have her thoughts diverted from her disastrous flying experience.

"Gray," she said, "would it be possible to make a short stop on our way to dinner tonight?"

"I suppose," he said. "What do you have in mind?"

"I have a key to the Wagner House," she said. "Have you ever been inside?"

"Well, no, but—"

"Then let me show it to you," said Erica, speaking with hopeful enthusiasm. "Since you've already agreed to hear me out about preserving the place, there's no harm in having a little guided tour, is there?"

"Somehow, poking around in a dusty old mansion is not my idea of a before-dinner activity," said Gray, his lack of interest evident in his tone of voice. "Besides, I don't care about the house—I only want the land it's on."

"Just give me twenty minutes," said Erica.

"How can you imagine that you're going to change my mind by having me wander through rooms full of cobwebs, peeling wallpaper, and moldy old carpets?"

"I thought you said you'd never been inside the place."

"I haven't."

"So how do you know it has peeling wallpaper and moldy carpets?"

"I just assumed that from the way the place looks on the outside," said Gray, with a knowing air. "That place is a wreck."

"Have I got a surprise for you," said Erica, chuckling into the phone.

"I doubt it," said Gray, with an air of profound skepticism. "If anything, your little tour is probably going to convince me that the house should've come down years ago."

"Give me twenty minutes," repeated Erica, crossing her fingers.

"Okay, I'll let you take me through the place," said Gray, expelling his breath. "But keep in mind that this is only going to hurt your cause, not help it."

"Let me worry about that," said Erica, and smiled to herself. In spite of Gray's obvious reluctance to step foot in the Wagner House, Erica refused to feel discouraged.

After all, she had a couple of tricks up her sleeve, which she would reveal all in good time.

"Here we are," said Erica that evening, as she and Gray pulled up and parked in front of the Wagner House.

They got out of Gray's car and stood on the sidewalk for a minute or two, silently regarding the building. Rising to three stories, the imposing old house was a turn-of-the-century creation featuring leaded glass windows, turrets, a peaked roof sprouting four chimneys, and masses of gingerbread trim.

Originally part of a residential area, the Wagner House was all that remained of what had once been one of Seattle's most prestigious neighborhoods. Now, the last of its kind, it stood alone on its weed-choked city lot surrounded by apartment buildings and small businesses. With its faded blue paint, a broken window here and there, and its sagging front porch, the Wagner House was a poignant visual reminder of a genteel age that had long since come and gone. The sight of it made Erica feel both sad and hopeful—sad because of its rundown condition and hopeful because she meant to change that.

"Let's walk around to the back door," said Erica presently.

She led Gray through a creaky iron gate and headed for a path that ran beside the house.

"I can't believe I let you talk me into this," muttered Gray, as they threaded their way through a wilderness of untended flower beds and encroaching ivy. There was debris everywhere, an unsightly littering of bottles, cans, wind-blown newspapers, and rusty piles of metal. A broken television lay on the overgrown lawn and an old washing machine leaned against one wall.

"What a mess," said Gray, kicking an empty cardboard box out of his path.

"Yes, unfortunately," said Erica, "when the owner died last year, people started dumping their trash here. But," she added brightly, "that'll be easy to clean up."

"What are you talking about?" said Gray, as they stepped onto the back porch.

"It's all part of my plan," said Erica, giving him a mysterious smile.

She fitted a key into the lock and pushed open the door. They went inside.

"And what plan would that be?" asked Gray, leveling his gaze at her.

"You'll see," said Erica and switched on a light. "Let me show you around first."

Later, at the end of their inspection of the house, Erica saw by her wristwatch that the twenty minutes Gray had promised her had turned into almost an hour. It had pleased her to note that, as they moved through the various rooms, Gray's demeanor had slowly turned from reluctance and a lack of interest to curiosity and finally to admiration.

Returning to the back porch, they paused while Erica relocked the door.

"Well, I have to admit," said Gray, "that this is a beautiful old house in many ways. The inside is not nearly as rundown as the outside. Still," he added with a laugh, "it's definitely what we call a fixer-upper."

"You really think it's beautiful?" said Erica, mentally crossing her fingers.

"Oh, sure," said Gray. "You don't see hardwood floors like that anymore, and those marble fireplaces must be worth a fortune."

"What did you think of the staircases leading up to the second and third floors?" asked Erica.

"Those are real gems," said Gray, taking her elbow and steering her off the porch. "I'll bet they're made of mahogany. Someone would pay thousands of dollars for the wood in this place alone, not to mention the stained-glass windows and those antique wall sconces."

Back at Gray's car, they settled themselves on the leather seats. Before starting the engine to drive to their dinner destination, Gray turned to Erica and spoke.

"Thanks for the tour," he said sincerely. "I had no clue what lay behind those decrepit walls. In fact, you've given me a wonderful idea."

"Yes?" said Erica.

She held her breath, wondering if Gray was about to tell her that he'd decided to rethink his plan to tear the house down. Was he now as sold on its charms as she was?

"It'd be a real shame," said Gray, "to turn a wrecking crew loose on a place like that—"

"Oh, Gray," said Erica, her happiness bursting through. "I just knew you'd change your mind once you'd seen the inside of the house. I just knew it."

"What are you talking about?" he said, with a small, puzzled frown. "I haven't changed my mind about anything. Once I own that property—and that's just a matter of time—the house is coming down. I've simply altered my plan a bit, that's all."

"What do you mean?" said Erica, her heart sinking.

"I was going to say," said Gray, "that before the wrecking crew does its job, I'll have a salvage company go in and strip the place of that gorgeous woodwork and marble and flooring." He started up the engine. "There's quite a market these days for building materials of that quality." The car pulled away from the curb. "I can't see sending good stuff like that to a landfill."

"But Gray," said Erica, appalled and disappointed.

"What?" he said, glancing over at her.

"Strip the house?"

"Well, sure," he said. "It makes sense to recycle what we can, doesn't it?"

"But that's part of Seattle's history," said Erica. "You'd ruin the place."

Even as the words left her mouth, Erica knew how ridiculous they sounded, in light of Gray's overall plan. She just couldn't bear the thought of workers ripping up flooring, dismantling fireplaces, and carting away the lumber from the staircases. It would be a desecration.

"The house is going to be torn down anyway," said Gray, smoothly negotiating a turn. "You and the other members of the Board of Antiquities will just have to get used to the idea."

"Never," vowed Erica under her breath, and stared out the window in frosty silence.

Chapter Eight

Twenty minutes later, Gray and Erica were seated in a cozy booth at Fontina's Italian Kitchen. Not wishing to cast a pall on their dinner, Erica put aside her feelings regarding the Wagner House, for the time being, as she shrugged off her jacket and looked around with approval. She'd never been to the informal little restaurant before and she immediately liked its comfortable, homey feeling.

Candles glowed in the warm dimness, spotless red-and-white-checked tablecloths and gleaming cutlery graced each table, and the air was redolent with the rich fragrance of herbs and bubbling sauces. The atmosphere was relaxed and intimate, and Erica noted with interest that the waitresses knew Gray by name.

"I like this place," said Erica. "Do you come here a lot?"

Gray smiled easily across the table at her. The candlelight bathed the chiseled planes of his face with an amber glow.

"Quite often," he said. "The food's wonderful, and it's a great place to unwind in after a long shift at the hospital." He chuckled. "For a single guy who usually doesn't have time to cook, Fontina's performs a very necessary function."

Erica pretended to study her menu, but her mind was suddenly on the subject of Gray's bachelor status. She wondered how he'd managed to stay single. A man as attractive and successful as he surely must've had chances to woo and wed any number of women. Then she remembered that he'd been engaged at one time. What was the story behind that? she mused.

She felt her brow wrinkle as her thoughts deepened. As she'd done before, she wondered if there was a connection between Gray's broken engagement and the woman who'd "paid dearly" for thinking of Gray as her hero. She stared at the menu items, but her eyes registered nothing but meaningless black lines scrawled across a white field. Although she did not want to pry into his personal life, Erica was naturally curious about Gray, especially since admitting to herself that she was more powerfully drawn to him than she'd ever been to any other man.

During dinner, Erica discovered that Gray's high opinion of Fontina's food was well-deserved. She savored every mouthful of the creamy mussel-and-tomato soup, the attractive array of vegetables on the antipasto platter, and the fettuccine verdi.

As they lingered over their meal, Gray kept Erica laughing and distracted with stories and humorous anecdotes about his travels. As she listened to Gray's tales, Erica's various concerns receded in the comforting atmosphere created by the romantic candlelight, Gray's attentiveness, and the excellent food.

Later the two of them shared a companionable lull in their conversation when espresso and chilled goblets of zabaglione were set down in front of them. A few minutes went by while they ate their dessert, then Gray broke the silence as he regarded Erica over the flickering candle.

"Tell me about flying today," he said, gently inviting her to unburden herself.

"I woke up with a bad dream last night," said Erica, "which got me to thinking that the longer I waited to fly again, the harder it would be. So I decided to face my fears and go for it." She raised her cup in a little show of bravado.

"You've certainly got guts," said Gray, nodding.

"But no glory, I'm afraid," she said wryly. "As you already know, my experiment was a huge failure." Just then, her emotions welled up in her throat and thickened her voice. "Aviation is my life, Gray," she said with quiet passion. "I've wanted to fly ever since I was a little girl. I'm not one to just sit back and wonder if I can do things—I have to go out and try them for myself. That's how I felt this afternoon, as if I was sitting around babying myself instead of taking some kind of positive action."

"I understand," said Gray. "So what happened exactly?"

"When I arrived at the radio station," said Erica, replaying the scene in her mind, "everything seemed fine." She shrugged. "I felt absolutely no fear at all, just a sort of tingling in the pit of my stomach, which I interpreted as excitement over the prospect of getting back in the air.

"It was great to see everyone again," she went on, smiling. "I spent about twenty minutes chatting with my friends there and thanking them for the flowers—that sort of thing. And then . . ."

"Yes?" said Gray. "Go on."

"Then," said Erica, taking a deep breath, "I asked one of the other pilots—a guy named Phil—if he'd go up in one of the choppers with me. You know, just in case." She gestured with her hand. "He said he would, and then he asked me if I was nervous about flying so soon after the accident."

"Were you, at that point?"

"I was starting to feel a few twinges, yes," admitted Erica softly. "But there was no way I was going to back down, and I just kept telling myself that everything was going to be fine." She lifted her chin. "So we went up to the helipad, did the routine safety check, buckled ourselves in, and up we went."

"With you at the controls?" said Gray, regarding her.

"That's right."

"And you felt okay?"

"Pretty much."

"So when did the panic set in?"

"About ten minutes into the flight," said Erica, and passed a shaking hand across her brow.

As she recounted the events for Gray, she was mentally reliving those moments of terror . . .

"Oh, no," she said in the chopper, and then could've bitten her tongue, for she hadn't meant to speak out loud.

"What is it?" said Phil, the sandy-haired man sitting beside her. He was looking at her with a curious expression on his face. "You okay?"

"I'm—I'm not sure," she said, trying to calm her breathing. It had increased its tempo, as if trying to match the sudden racing of her heart.

"Want me to take over?"

"No, no, I'll be fine," said Erica quickly. "It was just a little dizziness, that's all. I'm okay now."

"You're sure?"

"Yes," she said with determination, while, at the same time, trying to ignore the fact that her palms had become slick with sweat. *Get a hold of yourself*, she sternly chanted inside her head. *You know you can do this.*

She continued steering the chopper on a route that took them over the Space Needle and on toward Discovery Park, high on a bluff overlooking Puget Sound. Erica concentrated on the instrument panel, keeping her mind on the dials and switches, and trying not to think about the fact that her stomach had begun to churn with fear. *I am not going to let this beat me*, she fiercely repeated to herself over and over. *I am not.*

A minute or two went by, and then she realized that she had been avoiding flying over the open waters of the Sound. That truly would be the test of her courage and resolve, so she had better face it. One at a time, she wiped her sweaty palms on her pant legs, then, gripping the steering mechanism more firmly, she adjusted her route and the chopper swung out over the water.

"How're you doing?" asked Phil. He was smiling his encouragement.

"Okay," was all she could say, for her heart was pounding in her throat like a fist.

She looked down and that was her undoing, for the sparkling blue water, dotted here and there with whitecaps and little sailboats, brought back to her in vivid clarity the day that she and Buzz had crashed. She gulped for air, felt beads of perspiration break out on her brow, and there was a tightening sensation in her chest. Before she knew what was happening, she felt her mind going blank. Through her mental fog came the sound of Phil's voice.

"Hey!" he shouted. "What're you doing?"

When Erica came to, she had the impression that only a few seconds had elapsed during her blackout. But it had been enough to send the chopper off its course; her hands had left the controls and were lolling at her sides. Phil was now flying the machine, aiming it back toward the radio station.

A flood of disappointment, mixed with embarrassment, swept over her. "I'm so sorry," she said, as unshed tears stung the corners of her eyes. "I could've killed us both." She shuddered and shook her head back and forth. "I can't believe this is happening. I'm so sorry."

"Don't worry about it," said Phil, shrugging it off. "Everything's okay. We were never in any real danger; I made sure of that. Just try to relax—we're almost there." He gave a rueful laugh. "I'm just glad you didn't try this on your own. No offense, Erica, because I've always thought you were a darned good pilot—one of the best—but you might want to stay grounded for a while. I don't think you're ready for this right now."

Erica mutely nodded in resigned agreement. As the chopper traveled through the air, she fought to stay awake and alert, and found herself swallowing over and over to keep from further humiliating herself by throwing up. Nausea swirled in her stomach, her heart was still hammering in her chest, and a feeling of claustrophobia had her in its grip. Again and again, she inwardly cursed her luck. *Why does this have to be happening to me?* her brain demanded. *Why, why, why?* Angry and more discouraged than she had ever felt in her life, she kept her eyes on the far horizon, not trusting herself to look down again.

Back at the heliport, Erica stumbled from the chopper and hurried to the ladies' room, where, for a moment, she thought she was going to be sick. Mercifully, the feeling passed. She splashed some cold water on her face, waited until the corridor was empty, then left the station through a back door and drove home.

"How terrible that must have been for you," said Gray, who had been listening attentively to her narrative. "I'm really sorry, Erica."

"Thanks for not saying 'I told you so', " she said, looking over at her companion. "But you were right," she admitted with a sigh. "I was rushing things. Maybe next week, I'll try it again and, well, we'll see then if my flying days are over or not."

Gray reached across the table and squeezed her hand. "You'll fly again," he said with quiet conviction. "You're going to conquer this thing."

Not trusting herself to speak at that moment, Erica instead gave Gray a tremulous smile of gratitude for his support. It was especially welcome in light of the fact that when they'd first met, he'd been critical of her plan to return to flying. She reached for her purse and took out a tissue.

Gray signaled for more coffee, thus discreetly giving Erica a chance to blot the moisture from her eyes. By the time the waitress had come and gone, Erica had reined in her emotions and recomposed herself. Gray spoke.

"I've just had an idea, Erica," he said, regarding her across the table. "I'm taking some time off this coming week. I was planning to head on up to the Cascade Mountains and get in a few days of backpacking. My destination is Cathedral Valley—it's a wild and gorgeous place. Why don't you come with me?"

"Backpacking?" said Erica in a doubtful tone. "Except for a couple of Girl Scout rambles in a town park when I was a kid, I've never done any hiking, let alone packed everything in on my back."

"Which is kind of my point," said Gray.

"I don't follow you."

"Here's what I think," said Gray, leaning forward. "In order to conquer your fears about flying, you need to build up some confidence. Anyone who can hike into the back country and experience the independence of carrying everything they need right along with them is bound to go home feeling renewed and confident." He paused. "I've seen it happen with troubled kids from the city, for example. The wilderness always seems to work a kind of magic on people." He laughed. "It's better than a shrink."

"I don't know," said Erica, still sounding dubious.

"Okay," said Gray, "I'll admit it's a shot in the dark, but what have you got to lose? At the very least, you'll get to see why so many people are in love with the Northwest outdoors. Think of it . . . the crackle of the campfire, the stars at night, the wind in the trees. You'd love Cathedral Valley—I just know it."

"Oh, all right," said Erica, laughing at his boyish enthusiasm. "I'll go with you, but—fair warning—I'm a total greenhorn."

"Just leave everything to me," said Gray. "We'll start tomorrow morning, if that's okay with you."

"Sure," said Erica, her curiosity aroused, but at the same time wondering what she had gotten herself into. Then she brought up the subject that she'd purposely tabled until after their meal.

"Gray," she said, "let's talk about the Wagner House for a minute."

"Go ahead," he said, leaning back in his chair. "I promised I'd listen." He raised one brow. "Just don't expect me to change my mind, that's all."

"All I ask is that you keep an *open* mind."

When he silently nodded his assent, Erica began sharing her thoughts on the matter.

"Before the accident," she said, "I did some research on the Wagner House. I was looking for evidence to back up the Board's case for preserving the house as one of Seattle's landmarks. What I discovered was very interesting."

"Go on," said Gray, his face expressionless.

"It turns out," said Erica, warming to her subject, "that the original owner of the house, Uriah Wagner, made his fortune during the 1898 Alaska Gold Rush."

"Did he strike it rich up there?" asked Gray, revealing a spark of interest.

"Not exactly," said Erica. "He never even went to Alaska. He stayed right here in Seattle and shipped supplies north, which were then sold to the thousands of men—and a few women—who were headed over Chilkoot Pass and on to the gold fields. It's ironic: The Alaska Gold Rush made Uriah Wagner a millionaire, even though, as far as we know, he never once panned for gold."

"Hmm," said Gray, nodding.

"He built Wagner House in 1900," continued Erica, "then he became one of Seattle's most active philanthropists. Although he and his wife had three children of their own, they also adopted several orphans and gave them a home. Wagner also established a scholarship fund, and he founded Seattle's first hospital."

"Really," said Gray thoughtfully. "I had no idea."

"Nor do many other people," said Erica. "Uriah Wagner was a quiet, unassuming person, apparently, for his name is rarely associated with his many good deeds. I had to dig pretty hard to find out about him." She paused. "On a personal note, I also discovered that, after Uriah died and the house had been passed down through the family, my great-grandfather lived in the Wagner House for a time."

"Is that so?"

"Yes," said Erica, "as a young man, my grandfather served the Wagner heirs as an apprentice bookkeeper."

"I see," said Gray, taking a sip of coffee. "So you have a personal stake in saving that old place."

"I do," said Erica, "but my family's connection to the house is just a minor footnote. The Board of Antiquities looks at the bigger picture, which is: Uriah Wagner deserves to be honored for his role in Seattle's early history, and the best way to do that is to preserve his house as a monument to his many good deeds."

"If the Board wants to honor the memory of Uriah Wagner," said Gray, "they can do so in any number of ways. I've already explained how valuable that piece of property is. The land has to be cleared so that modern good deeds can go forward."

"Which brings up my next point," said Erica. "Did you know that the apartment building across from the Wagner House is for sale?"

"No," said Gray, with a little frown, "but what does that have to do with anything? I'm not interested in apartments. I'm trying to make space for doctors' offices and a new crisis clinic. I've already had an architect draw up a design for the new building."

"Just hear me out," said Erica. "Why not buy that apartment complex, which is already standing, convert it into office space, and—here's the best part—refurbish the Wagner House and turn it into a new crisis clinic."

"You can't be serious," said Gray. "Bringing that old house up to code would cost a fortune."

"Not if you do it my way," said Erica, smiling.

"Which means?"

"Which means," she said, "that an industrial arts teacher at Seattle Community College has tentatively agreed to take on the Wagner House as a class project. His students will clean up the grounds, rewire the place, paint it, replumb it—the works. They'll get practical experience plus college credit, and the cost to you will be minimal. There are even some tax breaks involved because the house is of historical importance." She paused. "So, what do you say?"

"I'd say that you've been quite busy behind the scenes," said Gray, quirking an eyebrow at her.

"All it took was a couple of phone calls and a stop at the college this morning," said Erica. "There are some details to work out, of course, but the plan is a sound one, in my opinion. It's a compromise that covers just about every base, don't you see?" She looked over at him. "Why don't you call your attorney right now, tonight, and ask him to look into buying that apartment building for you."

"Whoa, slow down," said Gray, with a touch of irritation. "I'm doing no such thing."

"But, Gray—"

"Look," he said, "I appreciate your passion, and I admire your—how do I want to put this?—creative thinking on the subject, but I have no intention of altering my plans." He held up his hand to halt her protest. "I'll make sure that the marble and wood and so on are removed from the house before it comes down. That's the best I can offer."

"So what exactly is wrong with my idea?" said Erica, determined to pin him down.

"For one thing," said Gray, "I'm in this deal with my cousin, and I can't imagine he'd want to make such a major change at this stage. It would take some pretty fast talking on my part to swing him around—assuming I'd even want to." He paused for emphasis. "Which I don't."

"What else?" demanded Erica.

"We'd be giving up floor space—"

"Not with the apartment building," Erica interjected.

"We'd have to relocate the people living in those apartments," said Gray. "Have you thought of that? What a hassle."

"Actually, I think that's already in the works," said Erica. "As soon as the building went up for sale, the city promised some relocation money. I'll check into that."

"Deals like that often don't go through," warned Gray. "As you know, money's a little tight right now." He paused. "And the part about the college kids. Oh, brother, that could be a liability nightmare."

"I believe that would be covered by the school's insurance," said Erica.

"But you aren't sure."

"No," admitted Erica, "but I'll look into it."

"Lots of loose ends," said Gray, as if he'd just rammed home the winning argument in a public debate.

"Tell you what," he went on, regarding her across the table, "I'll show you the architect's plan for the new building. I think you'll agree with me that it's a beautiful design and will be a great addition to the neighborhood."

"I'm really not interested," said Erica, with a touch of impatience. Her tone of voice revealed her frustration over Gray's many objections to her idea.

"Well," responded Gray mildly, "if you change your mind, just let me know."

"Gray, won't you please at least—"

"Could we table this discussion for now?" said Gray. "I gave you a fair shot at convincing me, but I'm not interested in your plan, and that's all I have to say on the subject." He regarded her. "It's pretty clear that I was wrong in thinking you'd come over to my side and then convince the Board for me. Why don't we agree that we don't agree and leave it at that. Let's not put a pall on the whole evening, shall we?" He reached over and briefly took her hand.

"Sweet Erica, I'd much rather just enjoy your wonderful company."

Gray's words, spoken so sincerely, warmed Erica's cool reaction to his disappointing rejection of her attempt at a compromise. She let out her breath and mentally took a step back from their conflict, but promised herself to return to the topic another time. Gray was wrong if he thought she would give up that easily.

"Oh, all right," she said, sending him a brief smile, "we can change the subject, if you like."

"Good," said Gray, "because I'd much rather talk about you."

"Me?" said Erica, with some surprise.

"Yes," said Gray, "I want to get to know you better."

"What do you want to know?"

"Oh, the basics," said Gray, a twinkle in his eye. "Your favorite color, where you grew up, and whether or not you've ever been in love."

Erica laughed. "Blue, mostly Denver, and no."

"Never been in love?"

"Oh, I've had my share of romantic involvements," said Erica, with a tilt of her head, "but nothing serious. Just waiting for Mr. Right, I guess."

Her little cliche was meant as a joke, but underneath it lay the truth, for Erica wanted very much to find a man with whom she could share her love. Gazing across at her dinner companion, she recalled how his kisses the day before had enflamed her senses. Being held in his arms had seemed the most natural thing in the world, as if that was where she belonged. She fumbled with her napkin, feeling awkward and confused that her mind could imagine an adversary in the role of a life partner.

"What about you?" she said, hastily turning the conversation around to focus on Gray. "Have you ever been in love?"

"Yes," he said, a guarded look crossing his face, "or at least I thought I was at the time." He paused. "In fact, I was engaged."

Erica studied him, realizing that, without meaning to, she had stumbled onto a topic that had made her curious ever since first hearing about it from Nurse Leslie.

"You know," he continued, half to himself, "I've never really talked about . . . all that."

"Maybe you need to get it off your chest," said Erica gently, sensing his need to do just that. "I'm a good listener."

Gray regarded her, an expression of vulnerability and remembered pain in his eyes.

"I think I would like to share it with you," he said, "but not here." He reached for the bill. "Come on, let's go somewhere else."

Chapter Nine

Fifteen minutes later, Gray and Erica parked at Alki Point in west Seattle and got out to walk. The rain-washed air had turned balmy, and the night sky was ablaze with gemlike constellations. Gray took Erica's hand and led her down some stone steps to the sandy shore, at whose edge lapped the waters of Puget Sound. The little waves made soft noises—*swish-swish*—on the dark and deserted beach, and, far off across the Sound, the twinkling skyline of downtown Seattle shone like a magical floating kingdom.

"Oh, look," said Erica, pointing out at the glistening ebony water. "There's a ferry. How beautiful."

Together she and Gray watched in silence as the huge vessel plowed through the night. The air was so calm and still, the mechanical purring of the ferry's engines could plainly be heard, even at a distance. Brightly lit and glowing, as if illuminated with a million candles, the ferry reminded Erica of an extravagant, many-tiered birthday cake. Its reflection slanted across the water, where it undulated like moonbeams shining through a prism.

Gray and Erica walked along the beach for a few minutes, saying little as they drank in the peaceful atmosphere. Presently they sat down on a driftwood log and stared out at the Sound. The poignant call of a seabird piped across the water, followed by the noisy flapping of unseen wings. Then all was silent again.

Erica held her conversation in check, having already decided to let Gray take the lead. She had the sense that he needed to work up some courage in order to bring himself to talk about his past engagement. Turning a little shell over and over in her hands, she wondered at that. It was hard to imagine Gray feeling fearful or hesitant about anything. After all, he was the man who'd risked his own life to save hers. She'd never known anyone as brave as he.

Then she stole a glance at him and her instincts were confirmed. Judging from the downward cast of his eyes and the furrows creasing his brow, he was indeed digging deeply for strength. Erica looked away, reflecting to herself that for Gray, personal disclosures might seem infinitely more risk-laden than any physical danger he'd ever faced. Soul-baring, she concluded, was not for the timid.

Gray cleared his throat and tossed a stone out at the water, where it landed with a little plop. *Okay, here goes*, his actions seemed to say.

"I was engaged a few years back to a woman named Lindy," he began. "I was just finishing medical school at the time." He paused. "Lindy . . . had a lot of problems."

"What do you mean?" asked Erica gently.

Gray picked up another stone and sent it hurtling into the night. "Emotional problems," he said. "Big ones. I didn't realize it until we'd been engaged for a while." He took a deep breath. "She'd had a pretty rough childhood, as I eventually found out. Her stepdad had been physically abusive to both Lindy and her mom. You can imagine how that affected how Lindy related to men as an adult. She was full of mistrust."

"How sad," said Erica. "Go on," she added, encouraging him to make a clean breast of it.

"She used to call me her hero," said Gray, a bitter note entering his voice. "She said that it was because of me that she had begun thinking that not all men are monsters.

"As time went on, though," he continued, "it became clear to me that marriage between us wouldn't work out. Lindy was incredibly possessive and very jealous. I wanted her to get some counseling, but she always had an excuse for not doing so. Eventually, I started feeling strangled by the relationship and, one night, I told her how I felt."

"How did she take the news?" asked Erica.

"Not very well," said Gray, softly. "I wanted to break off our engagement, but she wouldn't hear of it." He paused. "There was a terrible scene. She begged me to stay with her that night, but I had a big exam the next morning and had to get some sleep." He shook his head. "I left her place, never dreaming it would be the last time I ever saw her. If only I'd known."

"Known what?" said Erica, laying her hand on his arm. "Tell me the rest, Gray."

"I later heard from one of her friends that Lindy had cancer," said Gray. "She'd found out that morning, but was apparently waiting for just the right moment to tell me about it. Then I dropped my bombshell in her lap, that I wanted out of our engagment." He took a deep breath. "It was all too much for someone whose personality was fragile to begin with. I'm sure she felt abandoned at the worst possible time." He cleared his throat. "That night, Lindy killed herself."

"Oh, no," said Erica, tears of sympathy over life's unexpected tragedies welling in her eyes. "But, Gray," she continued, "you mustn't blame yourself. You do blame yourself, don't you?"

"Of course I do," said Gray harshly, as he wiped some angry, unshed tears from his own eyes. "I feel incredibly responsible for what happened to Lindy. I let another human being down when she most needed me."

"But it wasn't your fault," said Erica, pressing closer to him. "It wasn't your doing. She was emotionally disturbed—you said so yourself. She made the choices of not getting counseling and of not confiding in you about her cancer. Please don't blame yourself for what happened."

"She called me her hero," he said softly, staring out at the darkened water. He grunted and threw another rock. "Humph, some hero."

"Gray," said Erica, deeply moved by his story, "you must let go of the past. What's done is done and it can't be changed. Stop tormenting yourself about something over which you had no control."

He turned to regard Erica, his face etched in shadow and the pale light from the stars. His forehead and cheekbones gleamed coolly, like a metal mask depicting the classical face of tragedy. Then he wordlessly slipped his arm around her shoulders and drew her close.

"You're a wonderful woman," he said presently. Erica could hear the emotion in his voice. "I've never told this to anyone before. Getting it out in the open has helped. I'm grateful to you for listening and . . . and for not judging me."

"I could never pass judgment on you," said Erica gently. "Why, you're the kindest, most caring and sensitive man I've ever known."

"Well, I'm not sure about that," said Gray, laughing briefly in self-deprecation. "But at least now you see why I didn't want you calling me a hero for pulling you out of that wreck."

"I inadvertently triggered some very painful memories for you," said Erica. "Your reaction puzzled me, but now I understand." She paused. "Thank you for being so honest with me." Then she leaned her head back and looked up at him. "But you are putting me in a rather tricky position, you know," she said, feeling a need to shift into a lighter mood.

Gray cupped her cheek in his warm hand and tilted her face toward him. His lips were hovering dangerously near.

"In what way?" he said, his breath fanning her skin.

"Well," said Erica softly, tracing her fingers along the strong line of his jaw, "if you're not my hero, what are you?"

He pulled her closer and Erica fancied she could feel his heart increase its tempo. For a moment, she regretted having asked such a leading question, but it was too late to withdraw it, for Gray's answer was already forming on his lips.

"I think I want to be your sweetheart," he said. His voice, rich with meaning, revealed his yearning. "You feel it too, don't you, Erica?"

"Feel what?" she said, her response a whisper.

"That we're meant to be together," he said.

With her heart suddenly brimming over with emotion, Erica twined her arms around Gray's neck and raised her lips to meet his.

Their kiss, which began as a gentle caress, soon flared with passion. Gray covered Erica's mouth with his, as if slaking a thirst that only she could quench. His arms encircled her in a protective embrace as he whispered sweet murmurings against her skin, and rained a string of warm kisses along her bare neck.

As they clung to each other, Erica instinctively knew that sharing embraces there with Gray, under the friendly stars, was an act of both healing and affection. Perhaps Gray was right; maybe they *were* meant to be together.

Just then, Gray lifted his head and seemed to be listening.

"Oh, oh," he said, "I think we've got company."

Two figures emerged from the darkness, slowly walking along the beach. A third shape, a bounding dog, ran back and forth across the sand. Presently, Erica could see that the moving figures were an elderly man and woman out airing their pet.

She and Gray broke from each other's embrace, then resumed their side-by-side seating arrangement, just as if, a moment before, they had not been locked in a passionate entanglement of arms and hands and lips. Erica self-consciously patted her hair back into place and tried to calm the agitated beating of her heart.

As the elderly couple drew near, Erica and Gray exchanged greetings with them. The little dog ran up to investigate, its wagging tail thumping Gray and Erica on the legs.

"Pepper!" called the man. "Pepper, come here!" The dog ran back to the man, who then addressed Gray and Erica. "He didn't get sand on you, I hope."

"It's all right," said Gray, pulling Erica to her feet. "We were just leaving anyway."

Erica giggled as Gray led her back to the car.

"What's so funny?" he asked, as he held the door open for her.

"We are," she said through her laughter.

"What do you mean?"

"We're like teenagers who've been caught necking on the front porch," she said. "I hope we didn't act too guilty."

Gray went around to his side and slid in beside her. Then he leaned toward her, one side of his face bathed in the pearly illumination from a street lamp. He traced the line of her jaw and kissed her lips. Then he glanced at his watch.

"I'd better get you home," he said, "if we're going to hike into the wilderness tomorrow. You'll need some rest before you tackle that."

At Erica's houseboat, Gray and Erica stood in the shadows on the back deck to admire the view and say good night to each other. The lights from the city cast shimmering bands of color across the waters of Lake Union. Here and there, portholes in sailboats at anchor glowed warmly, like friendly amber eyes. The sky seemed especially vast that night, as high and wide as a black velvet awning stitched with crystalline starbeads.

Gray and Erica clung to each other, their mouths merged in a heart-stopping kiss of the sort that can go on forever. Finally Gray broke the delicious bonding of their lips.

"And now I really *am* going," he said, chuckling, his tone revealing that staying wrapped in Erica's arms was truly his preference.

Hand in hand, Gray and Erica walked over to the float. They paused, each dragging out the moments. Gray raised Erica's hand to his lips and kissed the sensitive skin on her wrist.

"Thank you for the lovely evening," said Erica, touching his cheek.

"My pleasure," said Gray. "Now get some sleep. I'll see you in the morning."

Erica watched him disappear along the floating walkway, then she went inside to prepare for bed. A few minutes later, she lay in her darkened bedroom and listened to the groaning timbers and the gentle splashing of water against the houseboat. By that time, a half-moon had risen. Beams from that cool silver body spilled through the window and cast a limpid swath onto the bedspread.

Unable to fall asleep right way, Erica sorted through the day's events, for much had happened since that morning. She'd faced the challenge of flying again, with unhappy results, and she'd turned a significant corner in her relationship with Gray. He'd entrusted her with a painful chapter from his past, and he'd revealed, through both words and deeds, his longing for her.

What a shame that the controversy over the Wagner House kept intruding on her thoughts, acting like a wedge that might ultimately keep her and Gray apart. Perhaps during their backpacking trip, Erica would be able to convince Gray to reconsider her compromise. She would give it a try, but she didn't hold out much hope. Judging from his reaction at dinner, he was unmoved by her pleas. If anything, he was more determined than ever to carry out his original plan.

Plumping up her pillow, Erica let out a sigh and willed herself to empty her mind of all such troubling thoughts. Tomorrow would have to take care of itself.

Chapter Ten

When Gray arrived in a Jeep the next morning to pick up Erica, who had attired herself in a cotton shirt and some comfortable walking pants, the sun was shining brightly. The clear blue sky with its smattering of puffy clouds promised a day of fine weather and caused Erica to feel cheerful and optimistic.

Even so, her stomach fluttered as she wondered what she had gotten herself into. As an inexperienced hiker, would she be able to keep up with Gray out on the trail? And what about the other not-so-wonderful aspects she'd always associated with backpacking? For a moment, visions of blisters, rain-soaked sleeping bags, and mice scampering through the tent danced in her imagination.

Glancing over at Gray as he drove, her fears were instantly stilled by the sight of his calm, handsome profile. There was nothing to fret about as long as Gray was with her, she realized, and turned her mind away from her worries.

Gray seemed deep in thought. She wondered what was giving him such a preoccupied air. Perhaps he was mulling over what he'd told Erica on the beach the night before. In the revealing light of day, was Gray regretting that he'd confided to her about his past? Erica hoped not, for she firmly believed that only through personal disclosure—sometimes of the painful variety—could true intimacy between two people be achieved. She admired Gray for having been so open and trusting with her.

Just then, he turned his head and regarded her. Reaching over, he took her hand.

"How'd you sleep last night?" he said.

His smile seemed to warm the space around them, and Erica felt a shimmer of pleasure in the pit of her stomach. She returned the squeeze of his hand. It was wonderful to be with Gray again.

"I slept just fine," she said. "I feel very rested."

"That's good," he said, looking back at the road, "because we're going to put in about six miles today, and that'll require stamina. But first," he added, turning a corner and driving the Jeep into a parking garage, "we need to make sure you're properly outfitted for our little expedition."

He found an empty slot, parked the Jeep, and he and Erica got out.

"Welcome to Trekkers," said Gray, "my favorite recreational equipment store. They've got everything. Come on, I'll show you."

Gray led Erica into a huge store that stocked every imaginable kind of outdoor gear. They walked through a forest of skis and ski poles, and explored a room where display tents of all shapes and sizes were set up on the floor. There was a section devoted to hundreds of books on outdoor topics, a room full of canoes and inflatable rafts, and an amazing array of hiking pants, chamois shirts, and leather boots.

Erica felt as dazzled as if she were Alice in Wonderland, for this was a whole new world to her.

"I can't believe this," she kept saying in awe, "I just can't believe it."

Gray chuckled, obviously pleased at her reaction. They stopped in front of a wall that was hung with neat coils of rock climbing ropes, pairs of metal crampons, and ice axes. Erica picked up a small object and showed it to Gray.

"What's this thing?" she inquired.

"Oh, that's an ice screw," he said. "It's for when you climb glaciers or frozen waterfalls during the winter." His eyes twinkled with teasing good humor. "How many do you think you'll need, a couple dozen or so?"

Erica hastily put the screw back down. "Did you say frozen waterfalls? I believe I'll pass on that activity for now," she said in wry understatement. "Lead on to the greenhorn section, please."

It didn't take them long to equip Erica for hiking and camping. Her purchases included a large backpack with several roomy compartments, a pair of sturdy boots and some wool socks, a suit of rain gear, a down sleeping bag, and some odds and ends that made her feel as if she could tackle any trail the Northwest had to offer.

"Whew," she said, as she and Gray stowed her gear in the Jeep, "I should be ready for anything now."

"Yes," said Gray, "you're all set. Just remember that, out in the wilderness, you must always expect the unexpected. That's why you'll be carrying your own compass and first-aid kit, for example."

"You know," said Erica, as she and Gray drove out of the parking garage and headed for the freeway, "maybe you're right."

"About what?"

"This might be just what I need to build up my confidence," she said thoughtfully, glancing at her pile of survival gear behind the seat. "Maybe after several days in the back country, I'll emerge a flyer again. I do so want this to work."

"So do I," said Gray sincerely, and gave her a reassuring smile.

An hour later, they arrived at the start of the trail leading to Cathedral Valley. They got out of the Jeep and spent the next fifteen minutes or so organizing their gear, lacing up their boots, and packing the food supplies that Gray had brought along. Then, after signing the trail register, they hoisted their packs onto their backs and started off.

They entered a cool forest whose dirt path soon began to climb. Erica was immediately struck by the fact that ordinary street shoes would not be up to such a task, and she was grateful that Gray had insisted she purchase leather hiking boots with sturdy soles. As she followed Gray up the incline, she often glanced down at the path, making sure to step carefully to avoid tree roots and loose rocks.

Later, on a long switchback, they paused beside a stream that was fed by a tumbling waterfall. As they rested with their packs off, Erica caught her breath and admired their surroundings. The sun filtered down through the broad limbs of the trees, casting warm patches of light onto the forest floor. Hidden birds twittered high in the canopy, and a squirrel with a twitching tail raced up a nearby trunk. Bright green moss flourished in the splash zone of the waterfall, and dainty white flowers nodded in the spray. The air was scented with the sweet perfume of sun-heated fir needles.

Erica smiled to herself, feeling calm, her soul at peace. It was good, she mused, to pause and soak up the tranquil atmosphere of the forest. She could already see why Gray loved being out there so much.

Gray's voice broke in on her daydreams. "Care for some gorp?" He was holding an open plastic bag toward her.

Erica thought she hadn't heard correctly. "Some what?" She eyed the bag with suspicion.

"Gorp," he repeated. "It's a Northwest trail snack."

"Why such a funny-sounding name?" asked Erica.

"Gorp actually stands for 'good ol' raisins and peanuts'," replied Gray, "but, since I made this batch myself, it has all kinds of goodies in it: Nuts, chocolate chips, dried fruit. Go ahead, try some. It'll get you up the trail to our next stop."

Erica took a handful of the mixture and began chewing. "Thanks," she said, "this is delicious." She looked at Gray. "How long will it take us to get to Cathedral Valley?"

"Oh, a few hours," he said. "We'll certainly be there before dark."

"Mmm."

Erica studied the toes of her boots and there was a long

pause. A breeze rustled in the fir boughs, a thrush fluted, and a couple of tree branches rubbing against each other made a pleasant singing sound.

"Erica," said Gray presently, "there's something I want to tell you."

He again offered her his bag of gorp. She distractedly selected some dried banana chips and crunched down on them. However, she barely noticed how crisp and sweet they were, because something in Gray's tone had put her on alert. Suddenly the atmosphere wasn't so peaceful anymore.

"What is it, Gray?" she asked.

She looked over at him, sitting across from her on a log. The strong planes of his face were patterned with dappled sunlight. Her heart missed a beat. Gray was so handsome, so appealing. Her whole being throbbed with sudden affection for him at that moment, and she recognized the possibility that she was falling in love with him.

"I may have told you," he began, "that my hectic lifestyle was going to change."

"Yes, I remember something about that," said Erica, nodding. "I'll admit you made me curious."

"Well, I didn't want to go into detail at the time," said Gray, "because nothing was final, but now it is. When I got home last night, after dropping you at your place, I found a message waiting for me." He paused. "Really, in a way, it's a dream come true. I've been waiting for a chance like this for years."

"A dream come true?" said Erica. "What do you mean?"

There was an expression of mixed feelings on Gray's face. He seemed pleased, certainly, but there was another element there that Erica could not put her finger on. Something seemed to be casting a cloud on Gray's good news, whatever it was. Finally, he took a deep breath and spoke.

"I'm resigning from the Center," he said.

"Resigning?" said Erica. "But why?"

"Because I'm leaving Seattle," he said. "I'm moving to Alaska."

Chapter Eleven

The bright sunshine that had been pouring down onto the trail like liquid gold seemed to flicker and dim, as if a giant hand had suddenly obscured the sky. There was a strained silence between Gray and Erica, broken only by the soft splashing of the waterfall and the raucous call of an unseen raven flying overhead. The bird's harsh cry made Erica shiver.

"You're moving to Alaska?" she said in a surprised voice.

"That's right," said Gray. "I applied for the position quite some time ago, and the paperwork has finally gone through. When I checked my messages last night, I learned that the job's mine. I thought the position wouldn't open up until fall sometime, but they want me up there in a couple of weeks."

"I see," said Erica, trying to mask her disappointment over Gray's unexpected disclosure.

Feigning nonchalance, she brushed some crumbs from her lap. She barely knew what to say, this was such sudden and distressing news. How ironic that just as she was admitting to herself that she was falling in love with Gray, he was about to drop out of her life.

She looked over at him. He was staring down at his boots, seemingly preoccupied by his thoughts. A lock of hair had fallen across his brow. Just then he raised his head and their eyes met, the expression on his face unreadable. His hand moved in a little gesture toward her.

"Let me tell you how this all came about," he said.

"I'm listening," she said.

"I've been a very lucky person," he began. "I was born into fortunate circumstances, I've had the best education money can buy, and I've been able to travel all over the world. But now," he went on, "I want to give some of that good fortune back."

"What do you mean?"

"For the last couple of years," said Gray, "I've felt somewhat limited at the Center. I've just had a nagging feeling that there was more I could do out there somewhere, something more challenging. So I started looking around for opportunities to practice medicine outside of the confines of a big-city hospital." He quirked a brief smile in her direction. "As you know, wild places call to me, so I concentrated my search in Alaska."

"And you found what you were looking for," said Erica, nodding.

"Yes," said Gray, "it seems I have."

A far-off look came over his face, as if, in his mind's eye, he was gazing on a vast and beautiful panorama of virgin landscape, devoid of scars wrought by human hands. Then he again focused on Erica.

"I've always been considered the rebel in the Moncrieffe clan," he said wryly, "so my news won't come as a surprise to my family. You see, what it boils down to is that I'm dropping out of the rat race. Part of me can hardly wait to do that."

Erica studied him, trying to imagine 'The Last Frontier', as Alaska was often called. She'd never been to that far northern state, but she'd seen pictures and movies about it. Her impression of Alaska was of a huge, untamed wilderness, rich in free-roaming animals and ancient glaciers crashing into the sea, and with a vast interior ruled by the four seasons.

Even more to the point for her, Alaska was a long way from Seattle. It was easy for her to identify the reason for her dismay over Gray's news. A fist squeezed her heart. Just as she was feeling a bond growing between her and Gray, he was slipping away from her. It didn't seem fair.

"What will your job be up there?" she asked, trying to keep her tone politely interested and conversational.

"I've signed on to be a bush doctor," said Gray. "There're a lot of remote little villages in Alaska whose people need more regular health care than they're receiving now. I mean to see that they get it. My home base will be in Sitka. I'll be living in a log house outside of town. I flew up to look at it this spring." He smiled at the memory. "It's nothing fancy, just a cozy, sturdy cabin with rustic furniture and a huge stone fireplace. It's on its own lake, where the fishing is terrific, I'm told."

"It sounds ideal."

"The agency I'll be working for," he continued, "will provide me with a pilot and a small plane. I'll fly from village to village, setting up a temporary clinic in each one so that I can treat those who need it. Prenatal care is one of my major concerns, plus I'd like to screen everyone's vision and hearing—you know, basic stuff. There's so much I want to accomplish.

"So you see," he concluded, "this is my chance to repay some of my good fortune. Plus, I've finally figured out how to combine business with pleasure."

"Well, I'm very happy for you," said Erica, trying to sound enthused, but her voice shook a little.

She was telling him the truth, but not the whole truth. Although she couldn't feel unreservedly joyful over Gray's plans for a new life and grand adventure up north, she did feel a measure of happiness for him. Love, after all, meant wanting the best possible good for the other person, a philosophy she had always embraced.

On the other hand, she longed to ask if he meant to return to Seattle someday, but the question stuck in her throat, as painful and prickly as a burr. Thinking about him dropping out of her life—and so soon—gave her a desolate feeling. She tried to shake it off, but it clung to her like a smothering blanket.

Suddenly, she felt overwhelmed by everything that was happening to her: the crash, the possibility that she might never fly again, and now this. Not for the first time in the last few days, Erica reflected that living a life took a lot of courage. At moments like this, she wondered if she was up to the challenge.

"Are you really glad for me?" gently probed Gray, his expression sober. "Or are you just saying that to be agreeable?"

"Yes," said Erica, and mustered a smile as she regarded him. "I'm truly happy for you, Gray. You'll be a wonderful bush doctor—they're lucky to get you."

She paused as another thought entered her mind, for she was searching for any silver lining that might brighten this dark cloud.

"Say," she said, "this probably means that you'll be dropping your plans for the Wagner House."

"Oh, no," he said, shaking his head, "I'll be turning most of the project over to my cousin Richard. I spoke with him this morning, and he assured me that he'll be happy to take on more of the details. Plus," he added, "we'll stay in touch and I'll continue to offer input. The project is still on."

"But Gray," said Erica, determined to press him on the matter, "you were just talking about repaying some of your good fortune."

"What does that have to do with the Wagner House?" he said, frowning.

"Here's your chance to help preserve a piece of the past," said Erica. "After all, there are some interesting parallels between Uriah Wagner and your family, if you think about it."

"Parallels?" said Gray. "I don't follow you."

"Both your grandfather and Uriah Wagner founded hospitals in Seattle," said Erica. "In fact, Wagner did it first. Surely, you must feel some kind of affinity with the man and his good deeds. And, if you do, it would be a wonderful gesture on your part to honor his memory—repay him, in a manner of speaking, for the good fortune he brought to the Northwest."

Gray let out his breath in a gust of exasperation. "Boy, you just never give up, do you?" he said. "I tell you about moving to Alaska and you somehow work in the subject of that decrepit old house."

"You can't blame me for trying," said Erica, smiling as she raised her chin with determination.

"No, I suppose not," said Gray, sweeping an impatient hand through his hair. "Well, let's drop the subject for now, shall we? It'd be a shame to argue on such a lovely day as this."

As the tension between them slowly dissipated, an expression crossed Gray's face that was difficult for Erica to interpret. She thought she saw a look of longing pass through his eyes, but she wasn't sure. Perhaps it was merely the play of sunlight and shadow filtering down upon him like little glass prisms, making everything seem to shift and change. She'd seen Gray emotionally exposed and vulnerable the night before, and she sensed a hint of those same qualities now. But, surely, he wasn't presently feeling vulnerable, not after sharing his happy news about Alaska. So why wasn't there a celebratory sparkle in his eyes? she wondered.

"You know," he said quietly, "this does rather complicate things in some ways I hadn't expected."

"What do you mean?"

"Well," he said, "I hadn't intended to get involved with anyone. I've known for some time that I'd be leaving—I just didn't know when." After a heavy pause, he went on. "So I didn't think it would be fair to any woman for me to—"

He stopped, exactly as if he'd come up against a wall and didn't know whether to turn left or right. He spoke again.

"It's important that you know how I feel," he said. "About you, I mean." He regarded her. "I think we're supposed to be together, Erica."

"Well," said Erica, brushing off her hands and standing up, "those are strange words coming from the man who's just announced he's moving to Alaska."

Gray apparently heard the edge in Erica's voice, for he also rose to his feet then quickly closed the gap between them. Taking Erica by the shoulders, he searched her face, holding her locked in his gaze. To Erica's dismay, she felt tears stinging the corners of her eyes.

"Gray, don't," she said, and looked away, biting her lip to keep from crying.

"Sweet Erica," said Gray, "listen to me. I've fallen hard for you—don't you see?—and I want to be with you."

With that, he pulled her against his chest and wrapped his arms around her. The cloth of his shirt brushed against Erica's cheek. A few tears trickled from her eyes, in spite of her efforts to hold them in check, and fell onto Gray's shirt. Numbly she watched the damp spots darken the fabric, flawing it like bruises.

"Darling," said Gray, his voice thickening, "we can work this out, I just know it. Please give me reason to hope that you want to be with me, too."

Then he lifted her face to his and kissed her. Uttering a

little cry of yearning, Erica twined her arms tightly around Gray and pressed herself against his broad chest. He smelled faintly of some kind of spicy soap, mixed with the pagan scent of bark and leaves and sunlight. Erica could feel his heart thudding in his chest. At that moment, nothing existed outside of their embrace as she returned his kiss, their lips mingling with pulse-pounding intensity.

"I never imagined I'd meet a woman who makes me feel this way," said Gray at last, stroking her cheek. "All I can think about is how wonderful it is to be with you, to hold you and kiss you and—"

Just then they heard the sound of voices coming down the trail. Gray and Erica turned to look as several boisterous children rounded a corner and headed their way.

"Oh, great," grumbled Gray at the interruption.

He and Erica stepped apart and moved off the trail, making room for the hiking party to pass. The children were followed by a tired-looking man and woman who smiled wanly at Gray and Erica. Soon the group disappeared around a bend and the noise of their chatter was absorbed by the forest. Gray glanced at his watch.

"Oh, well," he said, "we should probably get going, anyway, or we'll have to set up camp in the dark." He reached over and squeezed Erica's hand. "We'll talk some more later."

Erica nodded mutely, in a daze of emotions, for events were happening faster than she could absorb them. She slipped her arms through the straps of her backpack and fell into step behind Gray, where she walked along in silent contemplation.

Chapter Twelve

An hour or so went by, during which Erica simply tried to clear her mind and let the natural environment work its peaceful, healing magic on her. The path continued to climb. She noticed that as she and Gray gained elevation, the forest gradually began to change. At the trail head, the woods had been of the mixed deciduous and coniferous variety. Higher up, the slopes were covered mainly with conifers: Hemlock, spruce, and fir.

The trees were also getting much bigger and more majestic, Erica noted, as they walked by several stout-trunked evergreens. She and Gray crossed a couple of rustic wooden footbridges over cascading streams, then the trail leveled off along a ridge line.

"Time for a little side trip," said Gray, calling back over his shoulder. "Come this way—there's a special place I want you to see. We'll stop and have another bite to eat there."

"Sounds great," said Erica.

By that time, she was ready for another break. Her feet were beginning to feel the effects of continuous walking, her back needed a rest from supporting her pack, and she was hungry for something more substantial than gorp.

Taking a trail that branched off the main track, they hiked for about fifteen minutes, then rounded a corner and began to descend. The way widened and the stones disappeared, leaving a smooth brown path that wound between some of the biggest trees they'd seen that day. The lofty sentinels reminded Erica of the redwoods of northern California.

A hush seemed to fall around her and Gray as they walked deeper into the grove of giants. There was almost no underbrush. Clumps of ferns grew here and there, and some velvety mushrooms had pushed up among the needles that carpeted the ground. The Elysian silence was complete except for the occasional call of a far-off thrush. The bird's song was both eerie and beautiful, a series of slurred notes floating through the forest, reminding Erica of a Panpipe being played in a natural outdoor theater.

Halting near a sun-splashed pool, Gray motioned for Erica to stop and take off her pack. Soon they were seated side-by-side on a large, flat stone. Erica gazed up at the broad limbs arching above them, with patches of sky showing through, as blue and unblemished as a robin's egg. It was a scene of such perfection, she felt a wave of pleasure wash over her.

"Well," said Gray softly, "what do you think?"

"This is an incredibly beautiful place," said Erica, looking around. "It feels like hallowed ground, as if we should be talking in whispers." She paused. "I love it out here."

"Does that mean," said Gray, teasing her, "that I'm turning you into a rugged outdoorswoman?"

"I'm not sure I'd go that far," she said, laughing. "Ask me again tomorrow morning after I've spent my first night in a sleeping bag."

Gray dug into his pack and brought out sandwiches and apples. He handed a sandwich to Erica and she hungrily bit into it. They ate in relative silence, speaking only occasionally and then about nothing in particular. It occurred to Erica that they'd both fallen under the spell of the tranquil old-growth forest, and had an unspoken agreement not to mar the atmosphere with any distressing topics of conversation.

Something about the surroundings reminded Erica of Gray's nature photographs that she'd seen hanging in the hospital corridor. She turned to regard Gray, who was quietly studying her.

"Penny for your thoughts," he said.

"I was just thinking about one of your pictures back at the Center," she said.

"The one of the black bears?" said Gray. "Hey, don't worry about bears. We probably won't see any, and, if we do, they'll be running away from us. They're very shy—you needn't be afraid."

"Thanks for the reassurance," said Erica. "I had been wondering if we'd see any large, toothy carnivores out here." She laughed. "Actually, I was referring to the one of the baby spotted owls. Did you take it out here somewhere? I love that picture—those fuzzy little owls are so cute."

"I did, as a matter of fact," said Gray. "Spotted owls love old-growth forests like this. I found that nest not too far from this very grove, so keep your eyes open. We might get lucky and see one of the adults. Thanks for reminding me."

So saying, he took some professional-looking photography gear out of his pack. His camera had a telephoto lens and a special filter, which he checked before setting the camera within easy reach.

They continued eating in companionable silence. A couple of times, Erica stole a glance at Gray. She felt so safe with him. It was a shame that he was moving to Alaska, just when she most wanted to get to know him better. Suddenly, Gray's excited voice broke in on her thoughts.

"Heads up," he whispered excitedly in her ear. He was reaching for his camera. "Here comes a spotted owl. Do you see it?"

Erica looked in the direction he'd indicated and caught her breath. A medium-sized owl—brown with white spots—was flying toward them. It landed on the broad limb of a hemlock tree about thirty feet away and stared down at the two hikers. Erica noticed that its eyes were as glossy as black plums and that its rounded face was a soft buff color.

As Erica drank in the sight of the lovely creature—one of the few wild owls she'd ever seen—Gray snapped several pictures. At one point, he brushed against Erica as he tried a different angle with his camera. The casual touch of his warm body sent a tremor sliding along Erica's spine. She continued looking at the owl, trying not to think about her reaction to Gray's touch and his pleasantly disturbing nearness. Then she realized that, even when they were not touching, Gray seemed to emanate a vibration—almost like a powerful and seductive fragrance—that reached out and enveloped her. Being with him was an intoxicating experience.

The owl stared back at the watchers and blinked its dark eyes. Then it launched itself from the limb, spread its broad wings, and began gliding away through the trees like a little brown spirit.

Gray leapt up and began clicking off more pictures. Erica stood, as well, noting with interest that the owl made no noise as it flew. Then she remembered reading somewhere that owls' feathers were constructed in a special way, so that when they flapped their wings, their flight was silent, the better to surprise their prey.

"Fantastic!" cried Gray as the owl vanished from sight. He put down his camera and turned to Erica. "That's the best view I've ever gotten of a mature spotted owl. Talk about being in the right place at the right time. Wow!"

Spontaneously, he threw his arms around her and lifted her off the ground in an unrestrained show of jubilation. Caught up in Gray's reaction, Erica wrapped her arms around him and hugged him in return. The friendly old grove rang with their laughter as they abandoned themselves to their delight.

Finally Gray set Erica back down onto the ground, but he kept his arms about her. With their bodies so close, Erica felt a tremor pass through her. Gray's hands molded themselves to the curve of her back as he pulled her to him for a kiss.

"Sweet Erica," he murmured.

When their lips broke free of each other, Erica saw a look of such longing in Gray's eyes that it was all she could do to keep from blurting out her feelings for him. Something held her tongue in check, however, and she was suddenly reminded of the magical flight of the owl. On silent wings, some unspoken words had just passed between her and Gray. In the three or four days to come, out there in the wilderness, perhaps those words would find voice. She would bide her time—there was no hurry.

"Come on, Gray," she said lightly and stepped out of his embrace. "We'd better keep walking or we'll never get there."

"You're right," he said, "let's hit the trail." He reached for his gear. "Before we go, though, I just want you to know something, Erica."

"What is it?" she said, buckling the waist belt on her pack.

"The best part about seeing that owl," he said, "was sharing the experience with you." He regarded her. "It wouldn't have been nearly as exciting if I'd been here all by myself." His eyes lit up. "I can't tell you how glad I am to be introducing you to the great out-of-doors. Come on," he said, starting off, "wait'll you see where we're camping tonight."

Several hours later, just before twilight, Gray and Erica arrived at their destination, a lovely primitive campsite near the base of a dramatic range of jagged peaks. Dropping their packs to the ground, they scrambled up to a mossy overlook, where they drank in the awesome beauty that lay before them.

Erica sighed with rapture. The Cascade Mountain wilderness spread as far as the eye could see, with no human structures—no roads, no buildings, no power lines—to mar the view. She and Gray had left the lights and the noise of the city far behind. Here there were only forested slopes, little wisps of mist rising from the hollows, a cloudless sky over all, and the far-off glowing orb of the setting sun.

"Welcome to Cathedral Valley," said Gray, squeezing Erica's hand as he gazed around. "What do you think?"

"You were right," said Erica. "This *is* a special place."

They stood in respectful silence for a few minutes, paying homage to nature's handiwork, then returned to their packs and began setting up camp. Soon the sun dipped below the horizon and the purple shadows of twilight began pooling beneath the trees. Gray and Erica put up the roomy tent, pitching it on a patch of soft grass, then they arranged their two sleeping bags inside it.

Later, as they shared a tasty meal of freeze-dried stew, which Gray had prepared on his camp stove, stars began to flicker on, one by one, in the darkening sky. Gray pulled a candle out of his pack and set it on a flat stone between him and Erica. He struck a match on the stone and touched it to the wick. The mellow flame of the candle cast a golden glow, instantly creating an oasis of cheerful warmth deep in the forest wilderness.

Erica finished her food and set her bowl to one side. She looked over at Gray. The candle flame sent amber fingers of light playing along the contours of his face. His wide brow was smooth and his eyes contained a faraway look, as if he were deep in thought.

"That was delicious," said Erica, referring to the stew.

"Haute cuisine," said Gray, laughing. "Just add water."

He put down his bowl and regarded her. "You seem to like it out here."

"Oh, I do," she said sincerely. "This is wonderful."

"It's even better than you think," said Gray, with a mysterious air. "How are your shoulder and leg muscles, by the way?"

"They're pretty sore and tired," admitted Erica, rubbing her hand across the back of her neck. "I'm going to sleep like a rock tonight."

"You know, a nice long soak in a hot bath would do wonders for those aching muscles," said Gray offhandedly, as he gazed into the distance.

"Stop it," groaned Erica. "You're torturing me."

"What if I told you," said Gray, "that you *could* have a bath tonight?"

Because of the dancing pattern of candlelight and shadow on Gray's face, Erica couldn't tell if he was teasing or not. But surely he must be joking, she thought.

"Is that a serious question?" she responded, with a laugh. "You must have a cruel streak for even putting such an idea into my head." She gestured with her hand, indicating the dense, dark forest that loomed all around them. "I'd adore a bath, but where am I going to get one clear out here?" She nodded toward Gray's camp stove. "Wait, I've got it. You're going to heat some water for me so I can splash away in my coffee cup, right?"

"No," said Gray, standing up, "that's not what I had in mind at all." He reached for Erica's hand and pulled her to her feet. "Come on, I have a surprise for you." He chuckled as he studied her face. "Say, don't look so skeptical. You said you wanted a bath, right?"

"Well, yes," she said slowly, "but I don't see how you're going to conjure one up out here."

"Trust me," he said, "and no more buts, my dear. Just grab a towel and your bathing suit and follow me."

"You really aren't joking, are you?" said Erica, her curiosity aroused by that time.

"Nope," said Gray, digging soap, bathing trunks, and a towel from his pack. "The water's waiting for us in a great big wonderful tub. You'll see." He located his flashlight.

"I am going to be so disappointed if this turns out to be a trick," said Erica, wrapping her suit in her towel.

"It's not," said Gray. "Are you ready?"

"I guess," said Erica, still sounding doubtful. "Lead on, oh, bath magician. This I have to see."

Gray handed Erica the candle and clicked on his flashlight. Then, crooking his finger at Erica, he cast her another mysterious smile and headed off into the darkness.

Wondering how on earth Gray was intending to produce a hot bath in the middle of the Cascades, Erica finally shrugged her shoulders and began following him along a narrow path. After about five minutes of walking, they rounded a bend and came upon a natural stone wall. They stopped at the apparent end of the trail and Gray turned to Erica.

"I think you're going to like this," he said confidently.

Erica looked around. "But I don't see any tubs of hot water." She tilted her head to chide him. "Are you sure this whole thing isn't just the result of an overactive imagination?"

"You," he said, pointing a finger at her in mock rebuke,

"are going to eat those words." He started forward. "Come on, the proof is right around the corner."

Gray then led her along the wall and beyond a jumble of boulders. They passed through a narrow opening and he shined his light ahead. Erica let out a gasp of delight when she saw the reason for Gray's mysterious but knowing air.

"Violà!" said Gray, making a grand sweeping gesture with his arm. "Welcome to Moncrieffe Hot Springs, set down here just for m'lady's pleasure."

"Oh, how wonderful," breathed Erica, entranced. "I can't believe it."

"Wait until you try it," said Gray, visibly pleased by her reaction.

"But how did you know about this place?" said Erica.

"My cousin and I accidentally stumbled upon it a few years back," said Gray. "It's not on the map, so, naturally, we had to name it after ourselves," he added with a self-indulgent chuckle.

"It's amazing," said Erica, in awe.

Gray took the candle from Erica as they walked forward to inspect the hot springs more closely. A rock cave with a seven-foot-high opening reached about twelve feet back into the hillside. Warm spring water bubbled up from below, forming a deep, inviting pool that extended out into the open air within a natural stone tub. Erica noted with pleasure that bathers could either soak inside the cave or out under the stars. Steam rose from the surface of the crystal-clear, slightly bluish water, and the walls of the cave were decorated with delicate ferns and clumps of velvety moss. The place was even better than Gray had promised, and Erica could hardly wait to lower her trail-weary body into the soothing, beckoning water.

Stepping into the woods separately to change their clothes, Gray and Erica soon returned to the springs clad in their bathing suits. Gray clicked off his flashlight and set the candle onto a stone ledge beside the pool. Now the only sources of illumination were the flickering candle flame and the cool silver moon, whose light spilled down through the trees. Sheltered by the dark, silent forest, the cave with its bubbling springs and indoor-outdoor pool was like a magical fountain of pleasure, an oasis of sensual delight. And they had it all to themselves.

Erica smiled to herself and felt a thrill of excitement. She was living one of every woman's secret fantasies, that of sharing a private Shangri-la with a devastatingly attractive man. It was wonderful beyond words.

She watched as Gray lowered himself into the pool with a little splash and a groan of pleasure. Binding her hair up on top of her head, she also slipped into the water, sinking down so that only her head was above the surface. Steam rose on the cool night air, and silver bubbles rising from the gravel bottom tickled along her bare skin.

"Oh, my goodness," she managed to say, and gave a sigh of delight. "I never knew that warm water could feel this good. I think I'm going to weep with ecstasy."

Taking a deep breath and slowly letting it out again, she felt herself begin to relax in the soothing waters. The temperature of the pool was just right, the night air was fragrant with steam, and it was a wonderful sensation to lie soaking under the stars in such mellow surroundings.

Gray was leaning against the other side of the rock pool,

about ten feet away, smiling lazily over at her. He'd ducked beneath the surface, and his dark mustache and hair were streaming with water. He looked like a mythical river god.

As Erica returned Gray's dreamy smile, she felt a deep sense of peace and freedom steal over her. All of her worries vanished into the night as she imagined that she and Gray were alone in the universe. Here in these healing waters, nothing could trouble them, nothing could intrude on their pleasure and contentment. Another long sigh escaped her lips as she luxuriated in the soothing sensations that were enveloping her like a fragrant balm. Gently waving her arms in the warm spring water, Erica surrendered herself completely to her surroundings. *This is paradise*, she told herself.

The water moved slightly as Gray crossed the pool to a spot beside Erica.

"You seem to be enjoying this," he said quietly.

"It's incredible," she murmured, wriggling her toes on the clean gravel bottom. "I think I could soak here forever."

"These springs are so remote and hidden away," said Gray, looking around, "that other people probably don't even know they're here." He regarded Erica. "Let's keep them our secret, shall we?"

"Absolutely," she said, returning his playfully conspiratorial grin. At that moment, she couldn't remember when she'd ever felt so happy and at ease.

Gray reached for the soap and lathered his head and chest. Then he sank under the surface again to rinse off the suds and came up squeaky-clean. The little bit of foam from his impromptu bath drifted away on a current leading to a small overflow, leaving the remaining pool-water crystal-clear again.

Erica watched Gray's activities with interest, registering small details, such as the way his chest hair formed little soapy curls against his bronze skin. He had a disturbingly attractive physique, one of toned muscles and smooth skin. As she admired the wet sheen on his body, and the way the mellow candlelight caressed its planes and hollows, Erica felt herself so strongly drawn to him that her breath was snatched away. It was powerful stuff, the attraction she felt for Gray.

Then she raised her eyes to his face and felt a twinge of self-consciousness. He'd caught her shamelessly staring at him. And judging from the knowing look in his eyes, he found her keen interest as provocative as she did. He held up the soap.

"You're next," he said softly. There was honey in his voice.

She reached for the bar, but he held it away, playfully taunting her with a slow smile that made her heart leap.

"Allow me," he said smoothly. Then he turned her around to face away from him. "Stand up," he said, "and I'll do your back."

Erica suddenly felt as if she were living in a dream. Steamy vapors, as from a potent perfume, seemed to envelop the two of them in a scene from an exotic pagan legend. Had she and Gray stumbled onto a magical forest, where sorcerers had transformed an ordinary pool into a lagoon of enchantment?

The friendly, sheltering trees seemed to whisper as Erica mutely obeyed Gray's command and rose from the steaming water. The warm liquid slid down her body, and the cool night air raised little goosebumps on her skin. Relaxing her arms at her sides, she closed her eyes as Gray began to soap her back. His strong, capable hands felt wonderfully warm and alive on her skin.

The soap smelled of spices and musk. Its intoxicating fragrance further intensified Erica's impression that she and Gray had stepped into a fantastic dreamworld. As her mind took flights of fancy, Gray's slippery, soapy hands rubbed the small of her back and kneaded the tired muscles in her neck and shoulders.

"Mmm," she murmured, as content as a purring cat, "that feels heavenly."

"Yes, it does," was his throaty reply.

Erica could tell from his tone that he was referring to the feel of her skin beneath his fingers and palms. Just then, she registered Gray's breath against her neck. He had dipped his head and was kissing the sensitive skin behind her ear. Her pulse quickened. Beneath Gray's hands, Erica's body had become incredibly alive and tingling. It felt as if his expert touch was massaging all of her nerve endings to the surface of her skin. She imagined that she was melting with sensual delight, and she craved more and more of Gray's wonderful touch.

"If I didn't already know what you do for a living," said Erica in a dreamy voice, "I'd swear that you were a masseur. Where did you learn how to do this?"

"Oh, I think it just comes naturally," said Gray, and once again lightly grazed her neck with his lips. "It helps to have such an appreciative subject," he added with a chuckle.

It was all too wonderful . . . Gray's magical touch, the

soothing *drip-drip-drip* of water from the cave walls, the soft swish of a light wind in the tree tops, the steam rising from the water's surface and vanishing into the darkness above, and the lingering scent of the soap. All of these sensations combined to fill Erica's awareness to overflowing. Her mind drifted away to another sphere, where smoky planets hurtled through space and time had no meaning.

Soon, however, a little breeze whispered across her bare skin and she gave an involuntary shiver.

"Getting cold?" asked Gray. His voice sounded far off, as if it were part of a dream.

"Mmm, a bit."

"Let's soak a few more minutes and warm up before we head back."

"Good idea."

They sank down into the water until just their heads were showing. Erica fanned the healing liquid with her arms and looked up at the stars.

"Thanks for the massage," she said, returning her gaze to Gray. "That was incredible."

"My pleasure," he said, smiling.

A few minutes later, they reluctantly hauled themselves up onto the bank and reached for their towels. Laughing softly, they rubbed themselves and each other dry. Gray playfully threw his towel around Erica and trapped her against him for some kisses. Pretending to protest, Erica struggled in his arms, then giggled as Gray tickled her neck with his lips and mustache.

By the time they'd slipped into the darkness to dress and gather up their belongings, the candle had burned low into a waxy puddle and the air had cooled. Back at the tent, they wasted no time in snuggling down into their sleeping bags. Erica yawned as, somewhere off in the distance, an owl hooted.

Sleepily, she whispered good night to Gray. Then she nestled deeper into her cozy cocoon and listened to the owl's call. It had a wild, haunting quality, one that ideally suited the surroundings and Erica's present mood. What a perfect ending to the day, she thought, as a warm feeling of contentment spread throughout her body.

As sleep stole over Erica, gathering her in its velvet folds, she reflected with regret that such happiness as she felt now was probably short-lived. What an irony that just as her heart began opening up to Gray, she was hit with the news that he was soon relocating to Alaska.

Erica's throat momentarily tightened as she pictured a future without Gray, for she would surely remain in Seattle to conquer her fear of flying and get her aviation career back on track. Gray had indicated earlier that day that the two of them still had things to talk about, perhaps conflicts to sort out. Erica doubted, however, that anything they had to discuss would resolve this latest turn of events. Even if they could agree on the issue of the Wagner House—still a major bone of contention between them—the fact remained that Gray was leaving Seattle. All things considered, it seemed unlikely that she and Gray had any future together.

Oh, but it was hard to let such worries overwhelm her just then, with the friendly sound of the breeze in the boughs over the tent, and Gray's reassuring animal warmth radiating from the sleeping bag beside her. Snuggling closer to his solid, slumbering form, Erica let go of her introspection for the time being.

"Tomorrow's another day," she murmured and drifted off.

Chapter Thirteen

When Erica awoke the next morning, all was still and peaceful, save for the faint twittering of birds. A lacy filigree of sun and shadow danced on the surface of the tent. Erica stretched then looked over at Gray, who was still asleep in his down bag. Raising herself on one elbow, she studied his face. His wide brow and the planes of his cheeks were smooth and untroubled. A lock of hair had fallen across his forehead and his breathing was regular and easy.

As Erica regarded Gray, a wave of affection for him swept over her. Holding her breath, she reached out and gently traced the strong curve of his jawline, noting with pleasure how his eyelashes cast dusky shadows onto his skin.

Studying Gray in secret like this, Erica mused that she'd never before met anyone like him. So much had happened between them since their dramatic first encounter, so many layers of their personalities had been revealed to each other. Not so very long ago, she reflected, she hadn't even been aware of Gray's existence; now she felt as if she'd known him forever. She was so very much in love with him. Looking back, she realized that she'd somehow known from the start that this might happen; losing her heart to Gray had been inevitable.

Just then, Gray's eyelids flickered.

"Good morning," said Erica softly.

Gray opened his eyes. His mouth slowly curved into a smile as he reached out his hand to cup the side of her face. Drawing her to him, he kissed her lightly on the lips, then gazed into her eyes.

"I can't think of a more wonderful sight," he said softly, "than waking up and seeing you first thing." He sat up and stretched, then regarded her again. "Well, did you sleep like a rock?"

"Oh, yes," said Erica, laughing. "The combined effects of hiking, soaking in that amazing pool, and your wonderful massage put me straight under. Thanks again, by the way."

"You're very welcome," said Gray, nodding as he accepted her words of appreciation. "You know, I'm really glad that you agreed to this trip," he continued. "It means a lot to me. We needed to get out of the city, away from the noise and confusion, and be together, just the two of us. There are too many interruptions back there, too many people competing for our time."

"It does get crazy," agreed Erica ruefully.

"All of those distractions," he went on, "sometimes make it hard to focus on . . . well, on the truly important things in life. Out here I feel as if the peace and quiet sweep the cobwebs out of my mind and let me see things more clearly. The wilderness gives me back my balance, my perspective. How about you?"

"I'm not sure," said Erica carefully, trying to read between the lines of Gray's little speech. "As you know, I've not spent much time in the woods, so all of this is new to me." She smiled. "I certainly like it so far."

"I was hoping you would," said Gray, "but I wasn't sure. In fact, I'll admit that I wanted to know what kind of a team we'd make out here in the wilds." He cleared his throat then, as if he'd just realized that he'd revealed too much about his private thoughts. "What I mean is, when you're out here away from it all, you get down to the basics. You have to trust each other and work together."

"Yes, I suppose your life could depend on it," said Erica. Then a thought struck her. "Say, what would we do if one of us got hurt out here?"

"Not to worry," said Gray, "I have a cell phone in my pack."

"A cell phone?" said Erica, laughing. "I'm surprised to hear that, after what you just said about the noise and chaos of the city."

"You're just right," admitted Gray. "It does seem like a contradiction. In fact, I usually don't carry a cell phone when I'm hiking. To tell you the truth, I hate the things. Then I got to thinking that I probably should bring one along on this trip since you're a beginner at backpacking. I'd never forgive myself if something happened to you out here and I was unable to call for help."

"Hmm, I see," said Erica. She was touched that Gray

had made this special concession out of a concern for her safety and well-being.

"It's turned off, by the way," said Gray. "I would never let the ringing of a cell phone intrude on such peaceful, natural surroundings—it would be so out of place—but it's there in case we have an emergency." He kissed her lightly and squeezed her hand. "But we're not going to have any broken ankles or bear attacks, so put your mind at ease.

"Now, back to the topic of teamwork," he went on. "Why don't you roll these bags while I rustle up some breakfast."

"What freeze-dried delight is on the menu this time?" said Erica, lightly teasing him. "Mind you, I'm not complaining—last night's stew was delicious."

"How about pancakes made with wild huckleberries?" asked Gray. "Made from scratch, I should mention."

"Terrific," said Erica. Then she added, "What's a huckleberry?"

"You really are an innocent, aren't you?" said Gray with a laugh. "Huckleberries are a wild cousin to the blueberry. They're sweet and delicious and they grow all around here. I'll be back in ten minutes with enough for our pancakes. Can you start the coffee while I'm gone?"

"It's a deal," said Erica. She was pleased at the prospect of taking on her share of the camp chores, and was looking forward to tasting her first wild huckleberries.

As promised, the berries studding Gray's expertly made pancakes were mouthwateringly delectable. Accompanied by crisp bacon and steamy-hot coffee, the breakfast was a culinary delight, made even more delicious by the fact that it was eaten in the fresh, open air. When Erica later hoisted her pack onto her back, her stomach was pleasantly full, her heart was happy, and she was eager to see what interesting discoveries lay before them that day.

"Ready?" asked Gray, after making sure that they had tidied up the area and removed all traces of their stay.

"Let's hit the trail," said Erica.

"Follow me."

During the next few days, Gray introduced Erica to some of his favorite wilderness spots. He showed her a high meadow where elk browsed among the heather. Later they scrambled to the top of a ridge to look at some mountain goats on a neighboring slope. While Erica admired the regal-looking animals, Gray took some pictures of them. On one memorable afternoon, they sat at a safe distance and quietly watched a black bear and her cub rip apart an old stump in search of grubs. That night, Gray and Erica fell asleep with the lulling sound of a waterfall in the background.

As the days passed, Erica met the various challenges that came their way with a positive spirit and a willingness to try new things and expand her experience. Just as Gray had predicted, her confidence grew each time she crossed a stream on slippery stones, picked her way through brambles, or arrived at the top of a set of switchbacks barely out of breath.

She took the personal inconveniences in her stride, as well, learning to wash up in glacier-fed rivers, sleep soundly on the hard ground, and hike without complaining even when her feet hurt or her gear became drenched in a sudden downpour. None of these things, however difficult or inconvenient, could detract from the joy she felt at being with Gray.

As they walked along the winding forest paths, often hand in hand, Erica sensed that Gray was trying to communicate something important to her. She knew how much he valued the natural wonders all around them. She was also aware that any woman who hoped to meld her life with Gray's would have to embrace those same values. Gray hadn't spoken of these things in so many words— except for his reference to teamwork—but Erica could tell that he was closely watching her reactions to their backpacking odyssey.

On the afternoon of their last night in the woods, Erica felt a keen sense of regret that they'd be hiking out of the wilderness in the morning. As she and Gray set up camp for the final time, on the edge of a large open meadow, Erica pondered her feelings. She chuckled to herself as she recalled how the deep shade beneath the trees had once filled her with a subtle dread of the unknown. Now the mingled light and shadow of the friendly forest beckoned to her, inviting her to explore the cool emerald avenues that wound between the trees. Her spirit and her understanding of the natural world had come a long way.

As Gray began unfolding the tent, Erica, deep in thought, laid out the cooking gear. By that time tomorrow, the two of them would be back in civilization. The hustle-bustle of the city suddenly seemed artificial and empty to Erica. She'd always thought of herself as a city mouse, but now she wasn't so sure about that. As she set up the stove on a handy stump, she silently vowed to make trips to the wilderness a regular part of her life from then on. Such sojourns back to nature fed the soul and fought off the demons of a rat-race lifestyle.

She mused over her transformation from greenhorn to confident backpacker and realized that she owed Gray her gratitude. All along the way, he'd shared mountain lore and survival techniques with her. Thanks to his patient tutoring, she'd even learned how to plot a course over unfamiliar terrain with the use of a map and compass. Proudly she'd accepted his praise over her being such a quick study.

"Well, that's done," said Gray, surveying the tent with their two sleeping bags visible through the front flap. He checked his watch. "Let's take a little stroll before dinner, shall we? There's a great spot I want you to see."

"Lead on," said Erica, happy to walk without the weight of her backpack.

The path climbed steadily until it broke out of the trees and followed the up-and-down contours of a rocky ridge line. Walking along the ridge, Erica suddenly felt that she was on top of the world, for she and Gray could see for miles in every direction. They paused to catch their breath, sitting on a slab of granite as Gray pointed out various major peaks in the Cascade Range, ticking them off on his fingers: Adams, Baker, Rainier, and the eruptive Saint Helens.

"Oh, my goodness," said Erica, looking around. "What an inspiring view."

"Yes, it is," agreed Gray, and again checked the time. "Say," he continued, taking his cell phone from his pocket, "I hate to inflict modern technology on this peaceful scene, but there's something I need to talk over with my cousin. It could wait until tomorrow, I suppose, but I'd really like to clear something up today. I can probably catch Richard if I call right now." He smiled an apology. "Sorry."

"Oh, that's okay," said Erica, made mildly curious by Gray's mysterious air. "I'll climb up to those boulders and give you some privacy."

"Thanks," said Gray. "Oh, and watch your footing. This slope looks pretty unstable."

"I'll be careful," said Erica and, using her hands to steady herself, began scrambling upward over the loose stones.

Before long, she was high above Gray. Taking a seat with her back against a rock, she looked down and could see, but could not hear, him talking into the phone. She wondered what could be so important that he didn't want to wait until tomorrow, when he'd be back in Seattle. Then she shrugged, for it was no concern of hers. Relaxing against the sun-warmed rock, she gazed into the distance and calmly drank in the natural wonders spread out before her.

A few minutes had gone by when Erica suddenly spotted a large bird soaring over the ridge. Recognizing the species by its snow-white head and tail feathers, she jumped to her feet and waved her arms to catch Gray's attention. She could see that he had completed his call by then and was replacing the phone in its case.

"Gray, look up!" yelled Erica. "A bald eagle!"

Reacting to Erica's urgent gestures heavenward, for the bird was disappearing fast, Gray set down the phone, and, shielding his eyes against the sun, peered up at the majestic creature as it glided across the vast expanse of blue sky. What a thrilling sight.

In her excitement, Erica momentarily lost her footing and her boots kicked free some pebbles that began bouncing down the steep slope. The moving pebbles appeared harmless at first, but, as they rolled, they began dislodging larger and larger stones along the way. These quickly gathered speed and momentum, taking even more rocks and dirt with them, until the entire surface of the hillside had begun to shift.

Erica watched aghast as, in the twinkling of an eye, a handful of tumbling pebbles evolved into a full-blown rock slide of dirt and boulders, a lethal mass that was now plunging downhill like an out-of-control freight train, with Gray directly in its path.

"Gray!" she screamed over the thunder of moving rocks. "Gray, look out!"

What a horrible, helpless feeling it was to witness the terrifying scene as it unfolded before her. Everything happened so fast, and there was absolutely nothing she could do to stop events, once they had begun. With the sounds of crashing rocks and her own screams filling her ears, Erica watched as Gray glanced over his shoulder with a startled look on his face, then leapt to one side and disappeared from view. A split second later, the rock slide crashed over the spot where he had been standing, covering the area with several feet of rocks and debris, and sending a cloud of choking dust into the air.

Even before the slide had completely spent itself, with the rocks coming to rest in a gulley below the ridge, Erica was scrambling down the slope, panic in her heart, for Gray was nowhere to be seen.

"Oh, please, oh, please," she cried, praying aloud that

Gray had been able to jump out of the way in time, but fearing that he had been buried by the slide. Tears began streaming down her cheeks.

"Oh, please let me find him," she sobbed. "Let me find him."

She barely recognized the slope now, the terrain had been so altered by the onslaught of falling rocks. When she arrived at the place where she thought Gray had been standing just moments before, Erica frantically looked around and began calling his name.

"Gray! Gray, can you hear me?"

There was no answer.

"Gray!" she called more loudly.

"I'm okay, Erica," came his voice, which sounded muffled. "I'm okay."

"Where are you?" she cried, looking around.

"Over here," he said, and scrambled from behind a rocky ledge. The ledge had apparently protected him from the rock slide, which had tumbled past him. Except for a coating of dust and a rip in his sleeve, he appeared to be unharmed.

They crossed the several yards that separated them and fell into each other's arms. With hugs and kisses, Gray soothed Erica's tears, murmuring endearments into her ear as he pressed her to him.

"Thank God you're all right," he said, with a catch in his throat. "I thought you'd been swept away by the rocks. What an incredible relief to hear your voice."

"I lost my footing up there," she sobbed. "Oh, Gray, I'm so sorry about causing that slide."

"Don't be silly," he said, brushing hair from her face. "It

wasn't your fault. It could've happened to anyone." He kissed her. "Besides, we're both okay—that's the important thing."

"Oh, Gray," said Erica, clinging to him, "I thought you were dead. I was sure I'd lost you forever."

"Darling Erica," said Gray, "you haven't lost me. I'm right here."

"Hold me, Gray," was all she could say for a moment, and nestled against his chest as her crying began to subside. "Please hold me."

"I love you, Erica," was his reply. "Sweet woman, I'll never let you go."

"I love you, too," she said, looking up into his eyes. "I love you, Gray, with all my heart. I can't tell you how horrible it was to think you'd been buried under those rocks. I thought you'd been killed."

"I'm very much alive," he said, smiling down at her. "And very much in love with you." Then he kissed her with a tender passion that snatched her breath away.

Several minutes went by as they clung to each other, reassuring themselves through the powerful medium of touch that the other person was, indeed, safe and sound. Finally, they slowly and carefully began making their way down the slope, holding hands, stopping now and then to embrace, and laughing together in celebration of life and love and their good fortune.

After dinner that night, Gray and Erica lingered over their tea as they stirred the embers in the fire and listened to the comforting night noises coming from the forest . . . the sleepy call of a bird at its roost, the rustling of a small creature foraging among dry leaves, a chorus of crickets.

"I can't believe how lucky we were today," said Gray as he regarded Erica. "That was a close call."

"I know," said Erica. "I was just sitting here counting my blessings. One or both of us could've been killed."

"Instead, there was no harm done," said Gray, staring into the flames. Then he looked over at her with a twinkle in his eye. "Unless you count my missing cell phone."

"What happened to it?" said Erica.

"It got left behind when I made a leap for that ledge," said Gray. "It's now buried beneath a ton of rubble."

"Oh, I'm sorry," said Erica.

"It's no big deal," said Gray, laughing as he shrugged off the loss. "I'm just glad it's the phone and not me under those rocks." He punctuated his sentence with a meaningful whistle.

"By the way," he went on, "I want to tell you about that call I made."

"To your cousin," said Erica, remembering.

"That's right," said Gray. "I was planning to surprise you at breakfast tomorrow. But, well, now that we've survived a rock slide together," he added with ironic humor, "it seems somehow fitting that I share the news with you to-night."

"What news?" asked Erica, her curiosity aroused.

"Do you remember my saying that spending time in the wilderness clears the cobwebs out of my brain?" said Gray. "And that it helps me find balance and perspective?"

"Of course," said Erica.

"Well, as we've been walking along the last few days," said Gray, tossing another stick onto the fire, "I've been thinking a lot about the Wagner House."

"Oh, that topic," said Erica ruefully, for she'd all but forgotten the controversy that still lay between her and Gray, a piece of business that was both unfinished and unpleasant.

"Don't worry," said Gray, smiling over at her, "I think you're going to like what I have to say. You see, I've had a change of heart."

"What do you mean?"

"I'm in love with you, Erica," he said earnestly. "Do you doubt that?"

"No, of course not," she said, equally sincerely.

"Well, I got to thinking," said Gray, "that only a supremely stupid man would let anything come between him and the woman he loves." He looked deeply into her eyes. "Darling, I called my cousin today and suggested not tearing down that old house, after all." He gave a short laugh. "I thought it'd be hard to convince him, but it turned out to be quite easy. Anyway, we're going to go ahead and pursue the idea that you had for the place."

"Gray, are you serious?" Erica could hardly believe her ears.

"I've never been more serious in my life," said Gray. "We're going to restore that house, with the help of those college kids, and we're going to make an offer on the apartment building across the street. I told Richard to call our attorney first thing in the morning and get things going. Between the two places, we'll create a new crisis clinic and have plenty of private office space. It'll all work out."

"Are you sure that's what you want to do?" asked Erica.

"Well, it's not the most efficient way to go about things," admitted Gray, laughing, "but I know we can iron out the details." He gazed meaningfully at her. "And besides, there are more important things in life than efficiency. Like I say, coming out here always gives me back my balance and perspective."

"Gray," said Erica, her heart overflowing with love and gratitude, "I'm just speechless. Thank you so much."

His response was to capture her hand in his and kiss her fingertips. There was a longish pause, then, as they sat in silence, thinking their own thoughts as they stared into the flames. Finally, Gray spoke.

"Sweetheart," he began.

"Yes," said Erica, thrilling to the sound of the endearment.

"Even though the Wagner House business is behind us," he said, "we do still have a bit of a problem."

"I know," said Erica, a note of sadness creeping into her voice.

"I don't relish the idea of a long-distance romance," said Gray, alluding to the fact that he was soon moving to Alaska. "How about you?"

"No, of course not," said Erica.

"Would you like me to stay in Seattle with you?" asked Gray in earnest. "Just say the word and I'll cancel my Alaska plans."

"Oh, Gray," said Erica, deeply moved by his selfless offer. "That's so generous of you, but I couldn't ask you to do that. You may never get such an opportunity again, and, besides, I know how much going north means to you."

"Being with you means even more," he said. "These last few days have shown me that."

"No," said Erica, shaking her head. "No, it's out of the

question. I can't let you give up your plans. This might be the only chance you'll ever get to live your dream. If you let this opportunity pass, you'll look back years from now and wonder what you missed."

"I suppose you're right," admitted Gray quietly.

"Of course I'm right," said Erica.

"Come with me, then," he said, taking her hand and pressing it to his cheek.

"Dear Gray," said Erica, "I don't see how I can."

"Why not?"

"You're assuming that I'll conquer my fear of flying," said Erica, "and there's no guarantee that I'll ever do that."

"You *are* going to conquer your fear," said Gray, regarding her.

"Such confidence," said Erica, her voice tinged with irony. "I wish I could have half the faith in me that you do. But that's a tall order when I think back to the terrible panic and loss of control I felt the last time I sat in a pilot's seat." She wiped a hand across her brow. "As determined as I am to beat this thing, I have to face the possibility that my flying days might be over. I'm not even sure I can be a passenger on a plane, let alone the pilot." She paused. "Still, I need to stick around and find out, one way or the other."

"I understand," said Gray softly, a hint of resignation in his voice.

There was a long, thoughtful silence, broken only by the crackling of the fire and the sighing of a light breeze among the upper branches of the trees.

"Well," said Gray, seeming to shake himself out of a bittersweet reverie, "it's late." He started banking up the fire for the night. "We're not going to solve all of our dilemmas tonight. Let's get some sleep. Maybe by morning, one of us will have come up with the perfect solution to the problem of how we're going to organize our lives so that we can be together."

"I hope you have a magic wand in that pack of yours," said Erica, trying to lighten their bleak mood with a little humor, "because that's what it'll take, I'm afraid."

"Hmm," said Gray. "Well, we'll see."

Although he was obviously trying to put up a positive front, his tone of voice told Erica that his true feelings were more in agreement with hers than he cared to admit.

It was on that discouraging note that Erica later snuggled down in her sleeping bag, longing for the blessed forgetfulness of slumber. But instead of drifting off as she usually did after a day in the out-of-doors, she lay awake long after Gray had fallen asleep. Listening to his regular breathing and to the soft night sounds outside the tent, Erica reflected that the previous days had seemed to cast a spell of enchantment over her and Gray. Their time in the woods had allowed them to forget their troubles for a while and simply soak up the wonders that surrounded them.

As their time together drew to an end, however, the realities of their situation had returned, demanding to be faced. It was wonderful beyond words that Gray had decided to call off his plans to demolish the Wagner House, and Erica was very thankful for that. Even though that impediment had been removed, the fact still remained that Gray was moving to Alaska and Erica was staying behind.

A few tears trickled from her eyes as she thought of Gray

dropping out of her life, perhaps forever, for she knew that a long-distance romance had little chance of surviving. How could she bear to be without him? She lay awake a long time, crying softly and staring into the darkness.

Chapter Fourteen

Early the next morning, Erica awoke with a start to the sound of moaning. She lay there for several seconds, stiff with alarm and hardly daring to breathe. She heard the noise again, louder this time. Was a bear nosing around their camp? Then she realized that the sounds were coming from Gray.

She sat up and looked at him. The pale light of dawn bathed his face with pearly luminescence, giving it an unreal appearance as if he were under water. Erica studied him more closely. Gray's skin was damp with perspiration and his face bore a grimace. He groaned again and clutched his side.

"Gray," she said in an urgent voice, and touched his shoulder. "Gray, can you hear me? Wake up. What's wrong?"

His eyes flickered open and he moistened his lips. "I'm

166

in terrible pain," he said in a rasping voice. Clearly, the effort to speak made his situation, whatever it was, even worse.

For Erica, it was profoundly startling—not to mention frightening—to be jerked out of a deep sleep and find herself confronted with an emergency. It was even more unnerving to see Gray—strong, resilient Gray—reduced to such shuddering agony. *Stay calm*, she told herself, *stay calm*.

"Pain?" said Erica, wriggling out of her bag. "What kind of pain?"

"Appendix," he said with difficulty. "My appendix. I . . . I think I'm in big trouble."

Erica felt the hair rise on the back of her neck. She swallowed hard and took Gray's hand.

"Are you sure it's your appendix?" she said. "That could be serious, couldn't it?" she added, hating the question and all that it implied.

"Two yeses," he said simply, as if saving strength to endure the next wave of discomfort. "I need to get to a hospital."

"Okay, tell me what to do," said Erica, rousing herself to action as she pulled on her socks and located her boots. "How can I help?"

Seeing Gray in such misery broke her heart. She lowered her head to his chest for a moment, suddenly bowed with the horrible responsibility that had unexpectedly fallen into her lap. Gray could die if he didn't receive medical treatment, and soon. He was obviously unable to travel, so he must somehow be evacuated from the wilderness and rushed to a hospital. How was Erica going to accomplish such a feat?

She cursed under her breath that her misstep the day before had caused the rock slide that had buried Gray's cell phone. If she had the phone now, she could call for assistance, but without it, she had no choice but to hike out on her own and bring back help. All right, then, so be it. Pulling herself together, she lifted her head and regarded Gray.

"Tell me what to do," she repeated.

Gray gave her some instructions.

"I'll be right back," she said.

She scrambled outside to fetch water and Gray's first-aid kit. Returning to the tent, she helped Gray take some pain pills, then placed his full water container within easy reach. Gently pillowing his head on a folded-up shirt, she next bathed his face with a cool, damp cloth, hoping to give him some relief from the pain.

Outside the tent again, she scurried around the camp, throwing some things into her bag and gathering a few additional items to put inside the tent for Gray's comfort while she was gone. Her mind raced. How ironic that by an incredible twist of fate, she was now in the position of saving the life of the man who had once rescued her from certain death. In the grand scheme of things, she reflected, it probably made a certain kind of cosmic sense. In any case, the weight of the task that the universe had handed to her lay heavily on her shoulders.

"I mustn't fail," she murmured under her breath, her voice catching. "Oh, please, please, I mustn't fail."

She slipped her compass into her pocket and crawled back into the tent with the topographic map that they had been using. Spreading the map out beside Gray, she pointed to a spot buried amid the numbered contour lines.

"We're right here, aren't we?" she asked him, confirming their location.

Gray nodded.

Erica's finger then traced a path to the northwest.

"Okay, if I take this trail," she said, "and cut over on this forestry road, I'll end up in Cathedral Valley again."

"That's your best bet," said Gray, with a little nod. "There's a boys' camp about half a mile up Harvey Creek." He pointed out the place to Erica. "They'll have a phone and you can call from there."

Erica quickly scanned the map. Cathedral Valley was such a long way off; so much precious time would be lost while she hiked there.

"What's this?" she asked, indicating an area that was much closer to their present location.

"No," said Gray, shaking his head, for he had apparently guessed her intentions. "Don't even consider it."

"It looks like a logging camp," said Erica, ignoring his protest. "They'll have a phone."

"Yes, they will," said Gray, "but you can't go there."

"Why not?"

"Because it's cross-country from here," said Gray, wincing with pain. "There are no established routes and it's very rough terrain." He again shook his head. "It's out of the question."

"But I could save so much time," argued Erica.

Gray stared at her, a flash of anger blazing in his eyes.

"I said forget it," he said. "It's a dangerous, crazy idea and I won't let you do it."

"I'll be careful," said Erica, folding the map. "Besides, I know how to use the compass now. You said yourself that I'm a quick study, remember?"

Gray raised his head with an effort. "I will not have you risking your life for me," he said, a harsh note entering his voice.

"You risked yours to save mine," Erica gently reminded him.

Gray sank back down, his energy sapped from the exertion of their disagreement. From the expression on his face, Erica could tell that he found her perversely stubborn, immune to reason, and thoroughly vexing.

She instantly regretted having added to his misery. It was bad enough that he was fighting physical pain. Hours of lonely, agonized waiting lay before him. How thoughtless of her to increase his worry.

"I'm sorry, Gray," she said, smoothing his brow. "Cathedral Valley probably is the best plan," she added, without actually saying that she'd go there.

Her words seemed to reassure him. Thankfully, she watched some of the anxiety drain out of his face.

"I'll be waiting," he said, with a little touch of satire. Then he took a long breath and gazed up at her. "How inconsiderate of me to have an attack of appendicitis out in the middle of nowhere. I'm sorry, Erica."

"Don't be silly," said Erica, fussing with his sleeping bag in an attempt to make him more comfortable. "You can't help it."

A guilty look crossed Gray's face. "The darned thing's given me twinges in the past," he admitted. "I've been meaning to have it out, but something's always come up."

Erica's hands stopped moving. "Shame on you, Gray," she lovingly chided him. "You're so busy taking care of everyone else, you've neglected your own health. How could you?"

"It was easy." His gaze slid away from hers as another wave of pain passed through him. "But you're right, of course. I should've known better."

Erica leaned over him, tears springing into her eyes. "It was horribly selfish of you to ignore your health," she said, with fierce tenderness.

A tear slipped from her eyes, caught the first rays of the sun as it fell, and came to rest on Gray's neck.

"Selfish?" he asked in a puzzled voice. He reached up to touch the dampness on her cheeks.

"Yes, selfish," she repeated, clutching his hand and kissing it with trembling lips. "You should've taken better care of yourself." Her voice broke. "For me."

"Darling Erica," he said with a little laugh, "how could I know that you were in my future?"

He became very still then, his expression grave, his eyes filled with emotion. Very deliberately, he reached up and grasped her shoulder.

"I can't let you leave," he said, "without telling you something first."

"What is it?"

"The last few days have been the happiest ones of my life," he said, with an intensity that touched Erica's soul. "Even if I die out here—"

"You're not going to die," declared Erica with a vehemence that made her shake all over. "I won't let you."

"Shh, it's all right," said Gray, calming her. "I don't

think I'm going to die. But if I were to," he went on, "I think I could let go peacefully, knowing that I'd just experienced the best days of my life." He paused. "You're what made them so wonderful, Erica. Sweet Erica."

"Oh, Gray," she whispered and smoothed his brow.

Gray pulled her down so that her cheek was resting on his chest, his arms clasped tightly around her. He stroked her hair with infinite gentleness.

"I love you, Erica," he said. "With all my heart."

"My dear Gray," said Erica, and raised her head to gaze into his eyes. "I love you, too." She covered his face with kisses, then she stroked his cheek and blinked back her tears.

"We absolutely must figure out how to be together," he said. "There has to be a way—" He stopped as another spasm of pain contorted his features.

"We'll worry about all that later," said Erica, reluctantly breaking away from him. She wiped at the tears that had leaked from her eyes. "I'm leaving now." Giving his hand a final squeeze, she added, "Hang on, Gray. I'll be back as soon as I can. Don't give up on me."

"I won't," he said in a whisper. "Be careful." Then he closed his eyes and seemed to drift toward sleep.

Ten minutes down the trail, Erica paused to focus her mind and get her bearings. To the left lay the path leading to Cathedral Valley, to the right, the unmarked route to the logging camp. She estimated that if she hiked steadily, she'd arrive in Cathedral Valley in six or seven hours. By going cross-country to the logging camp, however, she could cut that time by more than half. She studied the map.

Gray was right; the terrain between there and the logging camp did look rugged.

Putting the map away, she knew, though, what her choice had to be. Time was the key element in saving Gray's life; every minute lost brought him that much closer to death. He was counting on her and she wouldn't let him down. Adjusting the weight of her pack, Erica left the trail and struck off cross-country.

For about an hour, she followed a series of ridges, pushing through dense thickets and now and then stumbling over exposed tree roots. At one point, she clambered to the top of a boulder to check her route with the map and compass. It was still early in the day, but already the sun was heating up the air. Erica wiped her brow, sipped some water from her canteen, and tried to catch her breath before continuing.

A woodpecker drummed on a nearby snag, the hollow sound matching the staccato rhythm of Erica's heart as she pictured Gray back in the tent, alone and in pain. She scrambled down from the boulder, skinning her elbow as she did so, and hurried on. There wasn't a moment to lose.

The going then became rougher as the landscape took a sudden dip at a ravine with a stream flowing deep at the bottom. Scanning her surroundings, Erica realized that she had two alternatives, neither one of which was ideal. She could either stay on high ground, following the upper edge of the ravine for over a mile and then backtracking, thus losing precious time. Or, she could plunge down the bank that lay before her, ford the stream at the bottom, and then climb up the other side.

She silently cursed as she weighed her options. The sun

was beating down on her bare head, for she had lost her hat a few minutes earlier to a sudden gust of wind that had blown it into some thorny bushes. Not wishing to spend time retrieving it, she'd left the hat behind and pushed on. Now she hastily tied a spare bandanna on her head and pulled it forward on her brow to give her eyes some relief from the sun's glare. Then she tightened the waist belt on her pack and began threading her way down the slope and into the ravine.

"Ouch!" she cried, as a willow branch whipped her in the face, its blow stinging her cheek.

Then she lost her footing and slid thirty or forty yards on her seat, ripping a hole in her pants. She was able to break her descent only by grabbing at a fir sapling that left sticky pitch on her hands. Getting gingerly to her feet, she pressed on, trying to keep her balance as she continued toward the bottom.

Once there, she scrambled to the edge of the stream and paused, scanning this way and that for the best place to cross. There were no handy stepping stones, so she just plunged in. The icy water reached halfway up her calves and made her gasp. Beneath the surface, the rocks were slippery—each step was a challenge. Halfway across, she fell to her knees, landing hard on one hand and drenching the front of her shirt. Once again, she cried out in pain and briefly flexed her fingers as she stood up and then felt a sharp twinge in her ankle.

"Please don't be sprained," she murmured out loud. "Oh, please, please don't be sprained."

On the other side, she stood dripping on the bank for a moment, catching her breath and reflecting on the fact that she must carefully balance the aspects of haste with those of safety. Although her ankle had twisted beneath her as she fell, it did not feel sprained. She almost wept with gratitude, for she was all too aware that if she did sustain a sprain or broken bone out there, Gray's only hope for survival would be gone—period.

Okay, stay calm, she told herself, and retied her bandanna with shaking hands. *You can do this. Just keep your wits about you.*

Looking around for the best way to ascend the other side of the ravine, she spied a meandering elk trail. She headed in that direction, stepped onto the rough path, and followed it steeply up the slope until it petered out. Next, she forced her way through a tangle of alder saplings, crawled under a fallen tree, and finally found herself, dirty and panting for air, at the top.

She quickly took another reading with her map and compass. Then she walked on, swatting at a large horsefly that was now buzzing around her sweat-stained face.

"Get away!" she cried and flailed at the annoying insect, which she knew could inflict a nasty bite.

The muscles in her legs were tired and aching by that time, and her stomach growled with hunger, for she'd had nothing to eat that morning. Still she forged ahead, ignoring everything except the urgent need to reach a telephone. Gray was waiting for her. The mental image of him lying helpless in the tent spurred her on and gave her strength.

Just then, she noticed a glossy black raven soaring above the trees. With ease and buoyancy, it rode the air currents and played the wind, completely at home in its element.

Then, giving its distinctive croaking call, it effortlessly sailed away.

If only I had wings, Erica thought, her heart squeezing. *If only I had wings.*

At last, she stumbled into the logging camp on weary, trembling legs. Heavy machinery and a cluster of maintenance buildings stood in a clearing. There was no one in sight. Frantically, Erica looked around. Where was everybody?

"Hey!" she called out. "Anybody here? I need help."

Just then the fragrance of coffee and bacon reached her nose. She followed it to the dining hall and dropped her pack onto the porch. Right before bursting through the door, she spotted something else in the clearing that made her heart pound with hope and excitement. A daring plan hatched in her mind, one that would require every bit of courage she could muster.

"Who's in charge here?" she said without preliminaries as she entered the building. "I need to borrow that chopper out there."

A dozen or so loggers looked up from their breakfast at the unexpected sound of Erica's voice. A man in a red flannel shirt, who appeared to be the crew boss, stepped forward and eyed Erica with mild suspicion. Erica knew she must present a bizarre spectacle, barging in out of the blue, dirty and disheveled, and demanding the use of their helicopter. They might think they had a deranged woman on their hands.

"I'm in charge," said the man. "Name's Norm Hilby." He paused. "And you are . . ."

"I'm Erica Johansen," she said, speaking rapidly. "I've

been out camping in the woods, and I need your help. You see, there's—"

"Whoa, whoa, slow down," said Norm, trying to calm her. "You don't look so good, ma'am. Are you okay?"

With a kindly but worried glance, he took in the tears in Erica's clothing, the soiled bandanna that had slipped off her head and was now hanging loosely around her neck, and the scratches on her forearms.

"And what's all this about using our chopper?" he added, looking puzzled.

"I'm okay," said Erica, "but there's a man out there in the woods who needs our help."

"What do you mean?" said Norm.

"He has appendicitis," said Erica, an urgent note entering her voice. "I left him in a tent, all by himself. He'll *die* if we don't get him out of there. Please," she said, almost frantic, "we need to hurry."

"I'm afraid I can't help you," said Norm, a frown creasing his brow.

"Why not?" demanded Erica.

"Our pilot's not here right now," he said, shaking his head. "He's in town, and he's the only one of us who knows how to fly that thing."

"It doesn't matter," said Erica, gesturing with her hand. "I'm a pilot—I'll fly the chopper."

"You?" Norm regarded her with doubt written all over his face.

"Yes," she said, then felt her features work themselves into an expression of appeal. "Please," she said, "we must hurry. I know I've caught you off guard, but I really am a pilot and I need to borrow your chopper to save a man's life." She clutched his sleeve. "You've got to believe me."

"Well . . ." said Norm, and seemed to be considering the matter. Then his demeanor became brisk and businesslike. "You'll need someone to go with you. Hey, Derek," he called to one of the men at the table, "come over here. We've got ourselves an emergency. You're going to go with this lady and help her lift a sick man into the chopper. Don't worry, she's a pilot."

A strapping young man with dark hair pushed his chair back and came forward.

"Thank you so much," breathed Erica to Norm.

"Happy to help," said the crew boss, and reached into his pocket. "Keys to the chopper," he said, and dropped them into her hand. "Good luck."

"Thanks," she repeated. "Please call the Moncrieffe Medical Center in Seattle right away," she added, as she and Derek started heading for the door. "Tell them to have an emergency team waiting for us at their helipad."

"Will do," said Norm. "Now get going, you two."

A couple of minutes later, Erica was sitting at the chopper's controls, Derek seated beside her. She hesitated briefly, her heart pounding in her chest. The last time she'd flown, she'd had another pilot with her as backup; this time, she was on her own. There was no room for failure.

"Are you *sure* you know how to fly this thing?" asked Derek. He was studying her with a tentative smile, as if wondering what he'd gotten into.

"Fasten your seat belt," was her confident-sounding reply. Then, taking a steadying breath, she engaged the engine.

They left the ground in a swirling cloud of dust. Urging

the chopper on a swift upward course, Erica soon leveled off and aimed the aircraft along an aerial path, back the way she'd come.

As she did so, an image of Gray—pale and wracked with pain—entered her mind. Completely focused on him, Erica acknowledged that a lot could've happened since she'd left him. Maybe when she arrived back at the tent, she'd find that she was too late. Refusing to believe that the worst had happened, she increased her speed.

"Be alive, dear Gray," she prayed beneath the roar of the whirling blades. "Please don't leave me now. Hang on, my darling. I'm on my way."

The next twenty-four hours passed by with a dreamlike sense of unreality for Erica. In a blur of urgent activity, she and Derek had bundled a semiconscious Gray into the chopper, flown to Seattle, and turned him over to the Center's emergency team. Feeling a mixture of relief and anxiety, Erica had watched as Gray was hustled into surgery. Then there was nothing to do but wait.

She maintained a vigil at the hospital, where a heavily sedated Gray was eventually moved out of surgery and into a private room. As he slept, Erica sat by his bed, holding his hand and, every few minutes, standing up to lean over and whisper words of love and encouragement into his ear. Whether or not he registered the sound of her voice, she did not know. Still, she had to do something, and it felt good and right to speak from her heart, even if Gray could not hear her.

The hours slipped by as Erica continued to sit there. Now and then, she rested her weary head against the edge of

Gray's bed, and sometimes she found herself weeping quietly with the awful fear that Gray might yet slip away from her. When a nurse gently suggested that she take a little break, Erica mutely shook her head, declining to leave Gray's side until she knew that he was going to be all right.

Late in the day, Gray's father and cousin Richard entered the room to check on Gray and introduce themselves to Erica.

"Ms. Johansen," said the elder of the two, "I want to thank you for saving my son's life." There were tears in his eyes. "He means the world to me—to our whole family."

Erica stood and shared an embrace with Dr. Moncrieffe, a tall, distinguished older version of his son. Overcome with emotion, she smiled up at him with trembling lips.

"He means the world to me, too," she said softly.

"Lucky man," said Gray's father kindly and squeezed her shoulder.

Richard spoke up.

"Flying him out of the woods like that took real guts," he said, a look of admiration on his face. "Thanks to you, Gray's going to live to tell the tale."

"Are you sure?" said Erica, her heart fluttering. She wiped her eyes and glanced from one man to the other.

"Yes," said Richard. "We just spoke with his doctor and found out that everything's going to be all right." He grinned over at the still-sleeping Gray. "My cousin here is going to be up and on his feet before you know it." He chuckled and shook his head with obvious affection. "The guy's indestructible."

A couple of hours later, Erica shared a few brief words

with a very groggy Gray. Feeling reassured that he was indeed headed for full recovery, she finally allowed herself to go home and get some rest.

The next day, she returned to the hospital, feeling revived and anxious to check on Gray's progress. She tiptoed into his room. He was alone and appeared to be asleep, his head making a dark-capped indentation on the pillow. Some of the color had returned to his cheeks, Erica noted with relief. She moved closer to his bed.

Many thoughts had tumbled through her mind as she'd waited to learn whether Gray would live or die. Some of her musings the day before had taken an unpleasant turn, in spite of the determinedly hopeful facade she'd maintained. If Gray died, she knew that the light would go out of her life. If he lived, though, she would be certain to tell him how much his parting words to her back at the tent had warmed her heart, fueled her courage, and given her strength for the difficult hike to the logging camp.

Gently she lifted his hand from the blanket, raised it to her lips, and kissed it. His eyes opened and he smiled up at her.

"Oh, dear," said Erica, "I've awakened you."

Gray squeezed her hand in surprisingly strong fingers. "No," he said, "I was only dozing." Then he pressed a button and raised the top half of his bed so that he could sit up. "I shook off the effects of the anesthesia a few hours ago. I've been pretty much awake since then." He pulled her closer. "It's wonderful to see you, Erica."

"Sweetheart," she murmured, and dropped a kiss onto his forehead.

"Say," he commented, a roguish twinkle in his eye,

"what kind of a kiss is that? Come here, woman, and do it right."

"But you're sick, Gray," she said.

"Not *that* sick," he growled playfully. "Besides," he added, "I suddenly feel much better."

So saying, he reached up and grasped her to him, kissing her soundly and passionately on the lips. The encounter made Erica's heart race, and she could feel a flush of excitement warming her cheeks.

"Oh, you really are feeling better," she said breathlessly. Her heart lifted with joy; it was wonderful beyond words to find Gray so brimming with life.

"Tell me something, Erica," said Gray, in a thoughtful tone. "Do you find it as interesting as I do that we've switched places?"

"What do you mean?"

"I saved your life and now you've saved mine." He paused. "My dad told me what you did. That was very risky, hiking cross-country to that logging camp. I certainly owe you my thanks." He paused then continued. "I don't remember much about that helicopter ride—I was drifting in and out—but I do recall that you were at the controls. What a woman. You've obviously conquered your fear of flying. Good for you, Erica."

"Thank you," said Erica, beaming in response to his praise, "but it was really just a matter of teamwork."

"How so?"

"You gave me back my confidence," said Erica, her voice laced with gratitude. "You took me out into the wilderness and taught me about survival and self-sufficiency. I'll admit that when I first got into the chopper, I had butterflies in my stomach." She grew sober. "But then I pictured you back in that tent, in pain and possibly dying, and I knew that I had no room in my heart for fear."

"Lucky for me," said Gray sincerely. There was a short pause, then a warm glimmer of good humor came into his eyes. "The fact that you've saved my life makes you my hero, doesn't it?"

"Now don't go all gushy on me," said Erica, in a teasing parody of what he'd once said to her. They both laughed.

"Well, anyway," continued Gray, "I'm grateful that you ignored my advice and headed for the logging camp, after all. I was in pretty bad shape and couldn't have lasted much longer in that tent. Thanks to you, I've been given a second chance at life." A film of moisture clouded his eyes for a moment.

"And now," he continued, after clearing his voice, "we have a decision to make, you and I."

"A decision?" she said. "What do you mean?"

"Back there in the wilderness, I told you I loved you," he said, "and I remember you saying the same thing to me."

"That's right," she said gently. "I love you with all my heart."

"Any fool can see that we're supposed to be together," said Gray, "so here's the deal: Either I am staying here in Seattle, or you are going north with me. Which is it going to be, Erica? Whatever you choose will be fine, because there's no way on God's green earth that I'm going to live without you."

There was a potent hush in the room before Erica spoke.

"I told you before," said Erica, "that I'm not willing to

ask you to give up your chance to be a bush doctor. It's a sacrifice I'm not going to let you make."

"You're coming north with me, then?" said Gray.

"Yes, I am," said Erica. "I've had lots of time to think while you've been lying here and that's what I really want to do." She kissed him. "I can't live without you."

"But what about your career?" said Gray. "You'd give up flying to be with me?"

"Maybe I won't have to," said Erica. "You told me that you'll be flying between villages in a bush plane."

"That's right."

"Well," said Erica, "you'll need a pilot for that, and—" she smiled through happy tears—"I just happen to be a pilot."

"What a great idea," said Gray, his smile broadening. "We'll make a wonderful team—you'll do the flying and I'll do the doctoring." He clasped her to him.

"Oh, say," he went on, with an exuberant laugh, "I almost forgot something in all of this excitement."

He reached beneath his pillow and brought out a small black velvet box, which he placed in Erica's hands.

"What's this?" she said. She traced the soft surface with her fingers.

"It's a present, darling," said Gray, looking as pleased as he could be. "Open it."

"But how in the world," inquired Erica, "did you manage to get me a present while you're lying in a hospital bed?"

Gray chuckled, obviously delighted that his surprise had caught her so completely off guard.

"About an hour ago," he said, "I called a friend of mine

and had him go to my apartment and get this for me. If it doesn't fit, we can have it altered."

"You're amazing," said Erica, slowly shaking her head. "How very thoughtful of you."

She opened the box and beheld a magnificent ring. Holding her breath, she gently lifted it from the little box with trembling fingers. It was the loveliest piece of jewelry she'd ever seen. Emeralds encircled an elegant diamond in a classic gold setting. As Erica admired the ring, its gems cast sparks of green and crystal-white fire onto the wall behind Gray's bed.

"Allow me," said Gray, and slipped the ring onto Erica's engagement finger.

"I—I don't know what to say," she said. "I'm so overwhelmed. It's the most beautiful thing I've ever seen."

"I inherited it a few years ago from a great aunt," explained Gray. "No one else has ever worn it. It's just been sitting in my safe, waiting for the right woman to come along. The idea came to me today that it belongs on your finger, Erica. I'm glad you like it."

"I love it, Gray," she breathed. "Thank you so much."

There was a delicious pause as Gray reached over and traced the line of Erica's throat with strong, warm fingers, lingering in the sensitive hollow where her pulse was fluttering like aspen leaves right before a dramatic change in the weather.

"Sweetheart," he said, "will you make me the happiest man in the world and be my wife?"

"Dear Gray," replied Erica, "of course I'll marry you." What soaring joy it was to say those words.

As Gray once more gathered her in his arms, emerald

fire from Erica's ring reflected in his adoring eyes. It reminded Erica of the green forest trails where her love for Gray had grown and flourished during their mountain odyssey.

Now, with twice the wonder she'd felt on that journey of the heart, she raised her face to him, as if to the life-giving sun. Like the mighty trees of the Cascades, Erica's love reached for the sky.